THE TIP OF MY TONGUE

AND SOME OTHER WEAPONS AS WELL

For Steve

TREZZA AZZOPARDI

THE TIP OF MY TONGUE

AND SOME OTHER WEAPONS AS WELL

NEW STORIES FROM THE
MABINOGION

SEREN

Seren is the book imprint of
Poetry Wales Press Ltd
57 Nolton Street, Bridgend, Wales, CF31 3AE
www.serenbooks.com

ISBN 978-1-78172-105-6
ebook ISBN 978-1-78172-107-0

A CIP record for this title is available from the British Library.

Cover design by Mathew Bevan

Inner design and typesetting by books@lloydrobson.com

Printed by TJ International, Cornwall

The publisher acknowledges the financial support of the Welsh Books Council.

Contents

New Stories from the Mabinogion

Introduction

Some stories, it seems, just keep on going. Whatever you do to them, the words are still whispered abroad, a whistle in the reeds, a bird's song in your ear.

Every culture has its myths; many share ingredients with each other. Stir the pot, retell the tale and you draw out something new, a new flavour, a new meaning maybe. There's no one right version. Perhaps it's because myths were a way of describing our place in the world, of putting people and their search for meaning in a bigger picture, that they linger in our imagination.

The eleven stories of the *Mabinogion* ('story of youth') are diverse native Welsh tales taken from two medieval manuscripts. But their roots go back hundreds of years, through written fragments and the unwritten, storytelling tradition. They were first collected under this title, and translated into English, in the nineteenth century.

The *Mabinogion* brings us Celtic mythology, Arthurian romance, and a history of the Island of Britain seen through the eyes of medieval Wales – but tells tales that stretch way beyond the boundaries of contemporary Wales, just as the 'Welsh' part of this island once did: Welsh was once spoken as far north as Edinburgh. In one tale, the gigantic Bendigeidfran wears the crown of London, and his severed head is buried there, facing France, to protect the land from invaders.

There is enchantment and shape-shifting, conflict, peacemaking, love, betrayal. A wife conjured out of flowers is punished for unfaithfulness by being turned into an owl, Arthur and his knights chase a magical wild boar and its piglets from Ireland across south Wales to Cornwall, a prince changes places with the king of the underworld for a year...

Many of these myths are familiar in Wales, and some have filtered through into the wider British tradition, but others are little known beyond the Welsh border. In this series of New Stories from the Mabinogion the old tales are at the heart of the new, to be enjoyed wherever they are read.

Each author has chosen a story to reinvent and retell for their own reasons and in their own way: creating fresh, contemporary tales that speak to us as much of the world we know now as of times long gone.

Penny Thomas, series editor

The Tip of My Tongue
(and some other weapons as well)

One

Sapphire Street
Summer 1976

...middle of something. It's a rare skill you have, Enid. Quite... unique.

My mother has stopped me asking my question by holding her hand up in the air like she's the lollipop lady on Splott Road. Now I have to wait while she feeds the curtain to the Beast, which is my mother's name for the washing machine which is not a real washing machine but is only a mangle. We have to do the curtains because the Erbins are coming, who are very rich and are relatives and have got a black dog. I know this because I am learning to be an International Spy and am gathering information by being sneaky and using my special powers to my Utmost Advantage as A Champion of Law and Order and Justice.

My mother always swears a lot when she does the mangling and always gives it the Look of Death and sometimes she even hits it.

A washing machine, he said, she goes, doing my father's voice, *Maria, I'll buy you a hundred bloody washing machines if it'll make you happy*. Give me strength.

I'd like to ask her my question but she has taught me that there are moments I can speak and moments I must Keep Schtum. My mother is training me to be a spy so that I can tell her what is going on with my dad when she is not there. I am her Eyes and Ears. She looks at me and her face is all pink and sweaty.

What? She says it like a dare, What now?

I can't ask her my question straight out as that is not how spies do it, so I make something up. This is known as a Cover Story and will put my mother off the scent.

Jackie says her little sister put her arm in the mangle, and she...

Don't you ever try that! she says, Don't you go near this thing! It's a tool of damnation. Stay. Away. From the Beast.

Up goes the hand again. She pulls the strap on her sundress and bends round the back of the Beast where the curtain is being spat out. The sun has burned her shoulder bright red. She's washing the curtains for the first time in Living History because my mother says the Erbins will look down their noses at us and say things like, Oh, your curtains are so disgusting, Maria, however do you stand it? Or they'll go, Oh, haven't you got shagpile? We've got shagpile in all our rooms and double shagpile in the bathroom too. And the dog has got shagpile wallpaper in his kennel as well.

We've never ever had a visit from a relative before, so this is the sort of thing we will have to put up with when they come.

By the time she's got the curtain out of the rollers, I have found a way of saying my question so it's not suspicious.

Will Uncle Horace come on his own? I go, all casual.

He's not your uncle, not technically. He's my nineteenth cousin fourth removed or something, and a toffee-nosed prat.

She stops and looks up like she's lost something and just spotted it again behind my head.

Christ Almighty, they'll want to eat, won't they? Go and get my tin, Enid, I'll need to have a think.

What she means is she'll need to have a fag because she always feels better when she has a rollie, and sometimes she lets me make the rollie myself with her machine.

Indoors the house is black as night so I can't see where she's put the tin at first, but then the lights go back on inside my eyes and I find it on the sideboard in the living room hidden under all my mother's stuff. There are lots of new poems on bits of any old thing all heaped up waiting for her Muse to come back.

My mother is Maria Bracchi, and she is also an Illustrious Poet, which my dad has told me means she is famous. Her real name is Maria Kilbride but when she married my father she became a born-again Italian, so she says, even though my dad's from Merthyr Tydfil. She is Illustrious though, that is really true because she's had her picture in the *South Wales Echo* twice and sometimes gets her poems done in little books. The Muse disappeared from my mother when she got the letter from Uncle Horace. My mother says her Muse is like a narky friend who can really help you but only when they want to.

She didn't show me what Uncle Horace had put in his letter, which I think is very strange as she wants my opinion on nearly everything, but I heard her telling it to my dad when I should have been asleep. Some of it I couldn't hear very well on account of the pipes under the floorboards, but most of it was about the weather anyway and what they do down in Devon where they live.

We so enjoy our trips to the coast, I don't know why you haven't considered holidaying here, she went, and then she said in her own voice, Because you've never bloody invited us!

Then she said something about their new Rover, which made me push my ear hard to the floor, because I know dogs are sometimes called Rover, and then she said more stuff about their visit, and then at the end she said:

...still have the black dog, is there any hope he will be free of it?

From my investigations I can conclude that:

1. The Erbins have got a black dog.

2. The Erbins have got a black dog they don't want and can't get rid of, even if they have got him a shagpile kennel.

3. We do not have a dog. Not yet.

Me and my mother sit on the step in the sunshine and she has a fag and I have an ice lolly from the freezer box and we both have a think about food. It's not that we are too poor or anything, it's only that my mother says she and the stove don't always see eye to eye. Everything she puts in the oven comes out looking like a tramp's shoe. So we're planning a meal that won't need too much cooking.

It's summer, Enid, she says, No one wants a hot meal in this weather. We can have salad and cold meats. And pickles.

Beetroot, I say, and we both look at the dirt where my dad will grow his vegetables.

Precisely, she says.

She puts her face on my shoulder and blows a big raspberry, and she smells of rollies and Aqua Manda and I can see how the freckles on her nose have all joined up.

Don't burn in this sun, lovely, get a bit of oil on, won't you? she says.

Do dogs eat salad? I ask, really sneaky. I will find a way to get my question out if it kills me. She looks at me a bit funny so I change the subject and say, Will Uncle Horace bring anyone else? like I couldn't care less if he does or he doesn't.

I expect Celia will be coming, so they're bound to bring Geraint as well. Can't leave him on his lonesome, can they?

Who's Geraint?

Their precious little bundle of joy, she says.

Is Geraint a name like Gelert? I ask, Or Rover?

My mother jumps up and goes through the kitchen door and when she comes back out, she's got the Famous Family Album under her arm. It's covered in cream leather with flowers on each corner which I know are called fleur de lys. I've seen every photograph in it, which are mostly of weddings or old people in grey hats and suits. There's one that's supposed to be of me but it's just a blob in a pram.

I like the ones of my mother and father best. In the first one it's their wedding day and they're standing together but with a rose bush between them and my mother is screwing her eyes up and my father is smiling really huge so his teeth are like tombstones. That was before he got his Dental Problems which have so Plagued him and Made his Life a Living Hell.

The other one isn't a very good photo on account of their heads being chopped off but you can still see my mother's swimming costume which is black and white stripes and there's a bucket and a spade and a sandcastle which she says my father spent all day helping me to make. Even though you can't see their faces, you can tell they're really enjoying themselves. My mother has put Monte Carlo underneath in joined-up writing, but one day she told me it was actually Porthcawl Beach and just a little joke because Carlo is my dad's name.

I don't remember being there because I was only little but I took this photo all by myself. Sometimes I try to see me in the picture with my bucket and spade, but I'm the one taking the photograph and you can't be in two places at one time. If you look really closely you can see the dents in the sand that I made with my feet.

My mother opens the album and gets a wodge of pictures out from the inside back cover.

Here they are, she goes, The perfect little family. Horace Erbin, his lovely wife Celia, and little Geraint in the shorts there.

Uncle Horace is wearing a suit with a gold chain on it to show how rich he is, and Aunty Celia's got on a hat so massive you can't see her face.

That's because of her squinty eye, says my mother, tapping the picture all disgusted.

I'm sad to see that Geraint is just an ordinary boy, apart from his hair which is black as coal and looks like the helmets they used to wear in the old days.

He's not like a Gelert at all. My mother can tell something has worried me because she puts her arm round my shoulder and gives me a cuddle.

I've told you, love, they didn't approve, she says. They made that perfectly clear. So they weren't gonna make it into the Famous Family Album, were they? But you can't hold a grudge for eternity, although God knows there's some that'll try.

What she means is there's a story behind the picture of my mother and father and the rose bush. I didn't notice it for ages and no one would ever guess, but once when we were going through the album when it was raining outside, she pointed to the rose bush and sang, Come out, come out, wherever you are! And I laughed because it's like she does when we play hide and seek, and she said,

See that little speck of white there, behind the roses? That's you. We wanted you in the pictures, but the photographer wouldn't allow it. So we found a way to sneak you in.

She thinks I'm worrying about me being born Out of Wedlock and all that, but I really couldn't care less about it, and then before I even know I'm going to say it, I say,

Will they be bringing their dog, too, Mam?

Two

My father's got a big black gap when he grins, right where his front tooth should be. He pulled it out with the pliers one Saturday after the racing when he couldn't stand the pain for one more second. With his gold earring in his left ear and his droopy moustache, he looks like Macoco the pirate. None of the other fathers round here look anything like a pirate, even though some of them have teeth gone, and according to my mother a few of them can walk the plank. He's waiting for a gold one to be made, but that was since before Christmas and now it's summer and he still has a hole big enough to put my finger in.

He works at GKN all week and on Saturdays he takes me into town to do the food shopping because my mother can't be trusted with money. Really I think he likes the fuss he gets from all the shop girls. We can spend a hundred hours buying half a pound of olives. Then he meets his buddies at the Hayes and he gives me his sugar cubes off the side of his saucer while they have their discussions. The thing to do with sugar cubes is to melt them a bit in your mouth before you bite them and then you can spread the crunchy bits all over the place with your tongue and later on in say maybe an hour when you've forgotten all about it you can find a bit of sugar snuck away behind your back tooth or up the side of your gum. Brilliant.

Once his friend Terence tried to give me his sugar as well but my father put a stop to it.

Don't do that, Tel mate, he said. She's addicted. And she's inherited my teeth n'all.

Terence looked a bit sorry for me with all my problems but it didn't stop him sneaking me a couple of cubes anyway when my dad wasn't noticing.

Sometimes I remember I'm supposed to be spying and reporting back to my mother, so I try to concentrate on what they're all talking about, but she isn't really interested in what I tell her, only how they looked. Was Errol's shirt ironed this time? Had Danny still got the plaster cast on his arm from when he got thrown out of The Rev? Was Michael wearing his wedding ring? That sort of thing. She calls it Doing a Recce.

There are masses of pigeons waddling round the snack bar. When I'm bored of spying for my mother I count the ones with bad feet. They walk like Mrs Millar from across the road. My mother says it's because she always goes out in her flip-flops.

Have you ever seen that woman in a pair of shoes? she goes, No!

Nearly all the pigeons have got toes curled up double or missing, but they don't seem to mind it.

After the Hayes we go to the indoor market and look at the animals in Gordon's pet stall. I'm crouching down talking to the rats while my dad is whistling at the parrot. He would love to have it, but my mother says she gets asthmatic around birds, and that's why I'm not allowed a dog. I know a rat is out of the question too.

The only allowable pet is a goldfish, but I've already had a few and they're very boring for a pet, going round and round and round all the time. The last one was black and yellow and we won it at Barry Island. My dad called it Moby after a famous shark when I wanted to call it Robert Crumb from two doors down on account of his mouth always being open like that, but my dad said how would I like it if someone called their pet monkey Enid? I said I wouldn't mind if I was allowed to play with it.

One day when I was at school my mother felt so bad for Moby she said she took him to the river and set him free. I didn't even notice for about a week, and when I finally saw he was gone, she said, See, that's why you can't have a dog. Left to you, the poor thing would starve to death.

I keep the *World of Dogs* book under my bed, which has every breed on the planet. I'd like a deerhound, which is like a cross between a horse and the sheepskin rug my friend Jackie's mum bought off the market, and plus their long faces remind me of Jackie as well. I think it would be nice to have a boy dog, and then I can call him David, after David Cassidy, who is an expert on puppies.

I'm considering Woody versus David as a name for my deerhound when my dad nudges me and points to the inside of the stall. Two puppies in a cage! They are batting each other with their paws and biting each other's heads. Close up they look like a couple of dishrags, both black and white with straggly fur and bits of straw stuck all over the place.

Gordon comes and points a warning at me. He's bald and fat and his head and neck are exactly the same size, and covered in tattoos, so from the back he looks like a giant marrow stuffed in a t-shirt. There's one of a scorpion crawling into his ear and more on his arms and hands as well, and knuckleduster rings on all his fingers. My dad calls him Gay Gordon, but not to his face, because he used to be a wrestler before he did his back in. Gordon won't let anyone put their fingers in the cages and there are signs up everywhere telling you not to as well, as if you'd disobey Gordon for one second.

What do you think your mam would say if we

came home with one of these? says my dad, crouching down and making kissing noises at the puppies. I think he's asking if I want one, but then I think about the one that'll be left behind with Gordon and I feel very sad for it.

Can't we have them both? I ask, and in that second he drags me away.

Just like your mother, he says, Offer the moon and you want the friggin' stars.

Back home, everything is in chaos. My mother lives her life in a state of Heightened Sensitivity, so it was bound to happen now the Erbins are coming. She has ironed the curtains and put them back up and now she's moving all the furniture round and putting the chairs in front of the curtains so that the Erbins can't see how much littler they've gone. That would be okay, except that the chairs were put where they were in the first place to hide the holes in the lino, so she's having to move the rug as well to hide the holes again. It's now at a squinty angle with the sofa, which I know will Unbalance her YingYang.

I can't see her for a minute because she's on the

floor behind the sideboard with a tape measure, saying numbers out loud.

Forty-eight and a HALF! she goes, By EIGHT-EEN!

On the bus home, my dad went into what he calls a Brown Dudgeon, which is a very dark and gloomy place inside his head. When it comes over him he has to go and lie down in the bedroom with the portable telly, a cup of tea and some rollies. Sometimes he can be in a Brown Dudgeon for days and stays upstairs with the curtains shut. Then the doctor has to come round and give him some pills. I'm worried that I've made it happen by being so ungrateful about the dishrag puppy, but at the same time I'm glad we didn't get it because my mother is building up to one of her moments.

My dad takes one look at the state of the place and goes straight upstairs. All the food is on the kitchen table still in the bags. I could make myself useful by unpacking everything and putting it away but there are three reasons in my head for not doing that:

1. My mother will want to see what he's bought,

especially if the Erbins are going to be eating it,
2. I'd need to get her to bring the stepladder out so that I can reach the high shelves in the pantry, and she'd just go, Chuh, might as well do it myself, and,
3. I get a wormy feeling in my stomach when they're both like this, like they've forgotten who I am or that I am even alive.

I get down in front of the sideboard and lay my cheek on the floor so that I can see her better. Underneath, right near my nose, there is dust, a penny, loads of beads, a hairbrush, and the sparkly bangle that came in my copy of *Twinkle* last summer. That's not even all of it. When I push myself under a bit more I can see bits of paper, a sock, some buttons, and two lipsticks, one with the top off. My mother's forehead is resting on the floor next to the skirting. She's stopped shouting out numbers and is breathing funny, so that the rolls of dust look as though they're running away from her mouth. She hasn't even noticed me under here: this really *is* like spying.

Why am I doing this? she says, Why? What's the point?

Then she turns her head and stares at me and her eye looks like a bright blue marble.

My daughter, she says, really quiet, Do you know how hard this is?

*

It's really great having the furniture in new places; you can play Sharks with added excitement on account of not being familiar with the layout. I'm playing Sharks now, but quietly, because my mother has gone to join my dad for a lie down. The Starting Line used to be the end of the kitchen mat so all I had to do was jump up on the arm of the sofa because it was right next to the kitchen door, and then I could Leap over objects in a Single Bound! Now it's in the middle of the room I have to use all my skills and go from the mat in one jump to the coffee table, then on to the chairs in front of the curtains, then do the sideways crab along the windowsill before dropping onto the sofa. I could even use the right-hand edge of the sideboard now that my mother has cleaned it up and put all her poems in the drawer. It could even become a new island.

Except she's also polished it, so it might be too risky unless I take my socks off. Sometimes when Jackie comes to play we do Shark time-trials. I think about how brilliant it would be if Sharks could be an Olympic sport, and after I've practised my route a few times I take off my socks and Increase the Level of Difficulty by doing a lap with my eyes shut.

Only, when I jump from the mat onto the coffee table, I forget about the ashtray in the middle and stub my little toe on it really hard. It's made of Onyx, which is like sharp concrete. I don't say anything but later on my mother goes,

What's all this blood on this table? and I tell her I had a nosebleed. It's never easier to lie but sometimes it's necessary for an International Spy, especially as she keeps telling us her Karma's out of Kilter.

Well, I hope you won't be having them when the Erbins are here, she says, We don't want them to think you're a health hazard,

which makes my dad laugh his head off. This is a good sign so I just try to forget about my toe and the noise it's making underneath my sock, which is a hot noise like boom, boom, boom.

In bed I lift up the blanket and have a look at my toe but I do it quick because looking at it makes it hurt more. It's black and red and the top is split so it looks like the lid on a trapdoor. I can't sleep for thinking about all the people in the brown dungeon trying to escape through the trapdoor. I can feel them banging on the lid, and at half-past something on my clock I hear one of them say, She's asleep, c'mon, let's do it while it's dark!

Three

My mother has made them all sit on the sofa, which is now in front of the curtains. She's also moved the rug again so that it's in Perfect Alignment with the edge of the sideboard, our new yucca plant is next to the fireplace, and she has covered the biggest hole in the lino with a massive cardboard box that she's filled with most of my toys and annuals.

My little toe was stuck to the sheet when I woke up this morning and looked as big as my big toe, nearly. I talked to it for a while to try to make it go down but then it felt like a thing I used to do before I became seven, when I thought everything could hear me even though it didn't have ears or a brain. I couldn't put my foot down when I got out of bed because after I tried it the first time I got an electric shock going up my leg and it's not something you want to happen twice. Now I know why the pigeons on the Hayes walk like that.

My mother was downstairs in the kitchen writing on a bit of paper and when she saw me limping she said, What's with the limp, honey? and I said, I'm being Tiny Tim, and she said, Well, Tiny Tim yourself back upstairs and get washed, they'll be here in an hour.

Then my dad came in through the back door with a huge plant in his hand.

Right, where d'you want me to put this, love? he said, taking the plant into the living room, and my mother disappeared and I could hear them discussing the plant, or actually, my father going, Are you mad? Who has a yucca in the middle of the friggin' room? They'll think we're mental.

Which is how my mother came up with the brilliant idea of the War on Want charity box.

★

Aunty Celia is not wearing a hat, but she won't look at anybody so I can't tell if her squinty eye is the left or right one. When she's asked a question, like, Do you take milk and sugar, she turns her head to one side as if there's a bad smell coming her way and speaks to the window. I think she must be very hot in her blouse and matching scarf, and her face make-up is so shiny she looks like she's melting. I'm also thinking they must've left their dog in the car out the front and she's worrying about it, but I can't ask her because, firstly, I'm to be seen and not heard, and secondly, I'm very worried that the boy Geraint is much too interested in the War on Want box with all my things inside it.

My mother says it's only a prop, but every time I see Sindy with her head poking out the flap and my annuals not in the right order I get a shiver going through me. *I'm* not allowed to touch them, but if the boy touches them there will definitely be War.

Just act nonchalant, my mother said, when she brought the box down this morning. She put it right over the hole in the lino, lit some joss sticks on the mantelpiece and straightened the ashtray for the millionth time. Then she went out through the back door and I had to let her in again through the front door and she stood in the middle of the room and looked all round and got the Glade out again.

You can have them back when the Erbins have gone, only don't go messing with them until then. Right? It's like we're setting the stage, Enid. We're going to be actors for a day. Remember the time that social worker came, and we played Little House on the Prairie? Well, it's just like that.

Are the Erbins going to take me away? I said.

My mother put her hands on my shoulders and looked me in the eyes. She always does that when she wants to treat me like an adult.

No one's going to take you away, she said, getting cross so the words came out very slow and hard, They are just visiting. We owe them nothing and we want nothing from them. But I want the place to look nice. Okay? Okay?

That's not what my dad says. He says the Erbins are well-off and we aren't, and if we make the right impression they might give me one of their ponies. That's what he said. When I said I'd really like a dog, but a big one, and showed him the picture of Woody David Marc Bracchi in my *World of Dogs* book, he laughed and said,

Looks like a pony to me, girl.

That was before we went to Gordon's pet stall, and he hasn't mentioned it since.

The boy Geraint is much taller than I expected and his hair is shiny black and stuck to his head and when he's not banging his knees together like he's wafting a secret fart, he's pretending not to pick his nose. If his finger goes anywhere near that cushion next to him he'll get a slap from my mother. My dad smiles a lot with his lips shut so they won't see the gap in his teeth and he says to Geraint, How's school? and Geraint goes: It's fine, thank you, sir. Then my dad says, Are you in the rugby team? and Uncle Horace says, He's more of a cricket man. He nearly made the Blundell's first eleven, didn't you, Gerry?

And then Geraint makes a little speech like this: I

prefer Fives, actually, sir. I competed in the under-sixteen National Fives and next term I shall compete in the Winchester Fives doubles tournament with Sam Cately.

None of it makes any sense to me, partly because his voice is going up and down and also because while he's saying it his eyes keep flitting over at my Dr Who annual. In the end even my mother notices and says,

Have a little look at that, Geraint, if you want. We're collecting for the starving babies, Celia. Boxes everywhere!

And she does a little fake laugh like it's a bit of a nuisance but no trouble really. Then she sees my face and she says, very rushed, Now, Enid, darling, why don't you go and show Aunty Celia the garden?

After I show her the garden – here are some flowers, this is where the vegetables can be – we both sit on next-door's wall in the shady bit. I don't show her the Beast, which is hidden under Tar Pauline which my father borrowed off Mrs Mickey's motor scooter last night, but if she asks I'm to say that it belongs to Mrs Mickey who has had to emigrate to Australia for a while and we're looking after it. I can't resist telling Aunty Celia about Mrs Mickey going away even though I'm not supposed to mention it, so I point to the Beast and say,

That's Tar Pauline, it belongs to Mrs Mickey next door. She's borrowed us her Yucca as well.

How nice, she says, It's very warm, isn't it, Enid? and she unwraps the scarf from round her neck. It's pink with silvery flowers on it.

That's better, she says, and has a sigh.

Are they fleur de lys? I ask, and she smiles all sunny and looks at me and I can see she hasn't got a squinty eye, it's just the left one's out a bit to one side.

Aren't you clever? Fancy you knowing that! Yes, they are. Look,

and she passes me the scarf and it feels like air going through my hands. She pats down the collar on her blouse and it's then I see she's got a hole in her neck, right in the middle. Even though I know it's rude to stare, I can't help it. It's like an ant hole, and then I'm thinking about the ants getting in and maybe we shouldn't stay in the garden too long because ants can move very quickly when they've set their minds on going somewhere.

What's that? I say, even before I think about not saying it.

It's a scar. I had to have an operation to help me breathe.

Can you breathe now? I ask, and she smiles again all sunny like before and says, Yes, thank you. I'm much better. What have you done to your leg?

I lift both my legs out in front of me and look at them. Clean knees. Check. Clean socks. Check.

Nothing.

I'm wearing my Scholls and new pink socks with the daisies on but my little toe has made the corner all black and red.

What's happened here? she goes, leaning over and pointing at the black bit on my sock, and when I try to hide it with my other foot she crouches down in front of me so that the hole in her neck is quite near to my eyes. It's not a hole close up, it's a black scab with pink all round it. She's trying to take my sock off really slowly and then she stops and says, It's stuck. Will it hurt if I pull it? but too late, because now I've seen what she's up to I yank my foot away and the sock stays in her hand and my toe starts bleeding again.

Has your mammy seen that? she says, in the voice adults use when they're trying to be calm. I don't know whether to say yes, of course, or no, she hasn't, because both of them sound like my mother doesn't care that my toe is falling off, so I don't say anything.

Aunty Celia takes a look around the garden for a minute and then she says, Just wait here, and she goes inside and when she comes out again she's got the Bottle of Danger in one hand and a cloth in the other and my mother right behind her. My mother's carrying her Tupperware bowl and her face is horrible, like it is sometimes when she's had one of her nights, all screwed up but with her eyes really staring.

My Enid, what have you done? she says, and falls on the ground in front of me so that the bottom of her dress is a ring of roses all around her. Aunty Celia kneels down next to her so it's like I'm the Princess and they are my Handmaidens. They both look at my toe for a minute and then my mother puts her finger underneath it and pulls it away from the other ones and looks at it a bit more. There's a wasp also very interested as it keeps whizzing between me and Aunty Celia and she wafts it with the cloth.

Kids, eh? says Aunty Celia, Never a dull moment.

Not with this little lady, goes my mother, splosh-ing the Dangerous liquid into the bowl and then dipping the cloth in, It's a non-stop carnival. This is going to sting, Enid.

I can bear it for a second because I don't feel it stinging at all, just cool, but then it starts to burn and keeps burning like it's burning a hole in my skin, like Aunty Celia's hole in her neck, and it's like she's reading my thoughts, because she puts her hand on my head and says,

Count to ten, Sweetheart, and it'll be better.

They both look at it again now it's been washed but I'm not looking, no way. I think the lid must be right off because the feeling is like fresh air getting in where it doesn't belong, like right inside you, and

I'm feeling a bit hot all over and the skin on my arms is bumpy like when you touch Crimplene.

You'll need a little bandage on that, says Aunty Celia, Where d'you keep your first aid box, Maria?

My mother looks up at her and squints and says,

First aid box? *First aid box?*

I know when she asks a question twice like that it means she's going to start, but she doesn't start, she just says,

Are you allowed a drink with your tablets, Celia? I could murder a cider.

Four

Geraint says that ants are like an army of soldiers and that in some countries they can kill you and that down in Devon an ant bit him on the arm when he was on the beach and when he went in the sea to cool it off he nearly drowned on account of the rip tide. Without me even asking he's telling me: A rip tide is a channel of water flowing seaward from the shore.

It sounds just like a poem, so I join in and do She sells seashells on the sea shore, but he bends his mouth down on the corners like I'm a baby to say that one, so I do Shut the shutters and sit in the shop, which isn't one of my mother's poems, it's one my dad learned me.

Candy is dandy but liquor is quicker, I say, which

is another one of my dad's, but the boy's already back on the ants, going on and on with his voice high and low, all about ant farms and scent trails and swarms and queens. I'm beginning to think he's going to be the World's Top Ant Expert one day and he'll be on the telly like Magnus Pyke.

My mother and Aunty Celia are sitting on the companion seat in the shade. My mother has a glass of cider and Aunty Celia has a Splott Pimms, which is like a cider but stronger, and they are talking quite quiet sometimes and then suddenly my mother will laugh. It's a nice sound, like the playtime bell at school. I have to pretend to listen to Geraint talking while spying on them at the same time.

Broke it in two places, says Aunty Celia, nodding over at us, And we didn't even take him to hospital! Thought he just wanted to get out of school.

Geraint has found my ice-lolly stick from the other day and is poking at the crack in the paving. He tells me to watch and in a minute I'll see something Quite Extraordinary. He is twice as tall as me but when he crouches down he is exactly the same size, only a bit shorter, so I can see where his parting is on his head and how greasy his hair is. His voice keeps going up and down and he coughs when it happens and starts again with whatever he is saying, which is mostly still about ants.

His fingernails are really long and absolutely filthy. When I ask him if he likes to play the guitar he gives me a funny look and carries on with his experiment. My dad grew his nails long when he was in the Easy Drifters, but only on the one hand so he could pull the strings louder. I'm going to explain this fact to Geraint when he says, Here we go!

He's made the ants so mad they've started running out of the hole and all over the path. He picks one up with his disgusting fingernails and carries it over to the bushes and says, Watch this, and throws it on the ground where it races round in circles on account of it probably having its leg squashed.

I didn't know it was going to happen otherwise I wouldn't have looked, but this spider dashed out from a web in the bush and jumped on it and then ran back like lightning. It made me feel a bit funny, seeing how quick it was, and I looked at Geraint's face to see if he was happy about it. My mother has taught me to try to be good to all God's creatures and even though I don't like ants, this looked like murder to me. But his face didn't seem to be enjoying anything.

That's cruel, I say, and walk away from him so that he can't say anything back, but when I get to the ants going mad over the path, I can't stop putting my Scholls on top of them all the same because I hate it when they try to run up your leg.

End of April, I hear my mother say, and for a minute I get rid of Geraint's voice in my ear and spy really hard, because April was when my mother went into the hospital. When she came back she went to bed for ages, maybe more than a week, and her arms were so thin she couldn't even open a tin of peaches. My dad would get me up in the morning before he went to work and then take me to Mrs Millar across the road, because his shift started at seven and school doesn't open until nine o'clock. Mrs Millar is fat and cuddly and she gave me sugar sandwiches for breakfast and coffee with hot milk which I'm not normally allowed. She's got a cat called Windy, and when I said, Is he Windy Millar? she laughed like a jelly and said, Dead right, girl! No flies on you.

I go and sit on the arm of the seat next to my mother so she doesn't keep talking about April and she starts doing that thing she does with my hair when she's having a chat with another adult, dragging it up from my neck and twizzling it round in a pile. She carries on talking to Aunty Celia about April but in a different way that she thinks I won't understand.

So, you know, we've discussed it and it seems for the best, given the circs with Carlo's depression and all.

And this would be when? asks Aunty Celia, with her eyes on me.

They'll let me know, says my mother and she leans over and pushes her nose in my ear and whispers to me, What are you up to, nosey?

And then to Aunty Celia she goes, But soon.

They're both quiet for a minute and then Aunty Celia takes a deep breath and says, Whenever, whenever you want, Maria. It'll be our pleasure.

Her eyes do a little flick at me as she says it, but it's a bigger flick than normal because of her left eye going out a bit. Before my mother can say anything else, Uncle Horace and my dad come out the back door and my dad says,

We're going to take the Rover for a spin round the block. Wanna come?

I'm first in line down the path because I want to hold his lead. Uncle Horace and my dad stand looking at the car for ages, walking round it and kneeling down in front and when my dad kicks the wheel, Uncle Horace says, Don't do that, old chap.

There's no dog inside. It's the car that's called Rover and it's a girl anyway. I'm getting that feeling like you get sometimes at Christmas when you wake up really early and open your presents and have all day left with nothing to look forward to until Easter.

Uncle Horace unlocks the doors and we all get in, Aunty Celia in the front and my mother and father and Geraint in the back, and my mother says to me, Come and sit on my lap, lovely, and my dad says, Squash up!

It's really hot in here already and there's a smell which makes me feel a bit hungry and a little bit sick. We go round the block twice and wave to the neighbours and then Uncle Horace says,

Shall we take her on the motorway and open her up?

And it makes me think about the lid of my toe and the ant in the spider's mouth and last April time with my mother with the bandages round her middle and my hair starts to sweat and before I know what's going to happen, it happens.

Oh God, Enid! Aw, Horace, pull over, mate! shouts my dad.

He's pushing me off my mother's lap and onto the pavement where I'm sick again. It's coming out red even though I've only had salad and boiled potatoes and bread and butter and orange squash and ice cream with a flake. My mother gets out of the car and says, I'll walk her back, you lot go on, but then my dad and Geraint pile out together. My dad is holding his t-shirt out away from his belly. It's got a bright pink splodge on it and Geraint is looking a bit white. He checks all over his shirt as well to make sure that he hasn't got any on him. Then Aunty Celia gets out of the front and says,

Let's just leave the boys to it, shall we?

My mother looks at my dad's t-shirt.

It's only a bit of beetroot, she goes, I'll get something to clean it off with later. You go on.

My dad jumps in the front seat but Geraint doesn't get back in, he walks away from us picking at the hedges as he goes past them. My mother tells me to go and catch him up. I've got beetroot sick down my dress and on my sock and my foot is going hot-hotter, hot-hotter every time it hits the pavement.

I don't want Mr Fish to come out and say, Oi! You! Leave my bloody hedge alone! so I'll have to move quick but it still takes ages to catch up with Geraint because he's got such lanky legs.

Are they for the ants? I say, pointing at his leaf collection.

What? he says, and looks at his handful and then just throws them on the floor like he didn't know what he was doing holding them.

Will you be going to Bramden? he says, Because you know, Blundell's only takes boys.

What's Bramdead? I ask.

It's a school, stupid.

Why would I go to Bramdead?

Bramden.

Okay. Why would I go?

He shrugs and starts ripping at the hedges again.

Because you won't be able to stay at home all day with mummy. You'll have to go *somewhere*.

Why can't I go to St Saviour's like I always do?

Because – well, I don't know, do I? he says, and rips a bit more hedge off from the next garden along.

I don't expect your father can afford it anyway, he says, He hasn't even got a car.

Yes he has.

What kind is it then? he says, and turns to look at me straight on so I can see he's got a touch of his mother's eye trouble.

It's a... it's a Gelert! I say.

That gets him thinking, because he's quiet for a minute and then he says, Where is it then?

It's in Australia. On a cruise.

He looks at me and starts to laugh in a funny way, like if a horse could laugh, then he shakes his head and laughs some more and it's beginning to get me a bit crazed.

Yah, right, he says, With his speedboat and his private jet. Your father's a gyppo. His teeth! My God!

The way he says My God is like this: Myyy Gord!

He's having a gold one made, I say, With diamonds in it by the queen's doctor. Ask him if you don't believe me!

You're not very good at lying, little girl, he says, and waggles a bit of hedge leaf under my nose so I get really, really crazed and before I know what to say I'm swinging my arm up and belting him under the chin. Next thing, he's got blood coming from his mouth and he's turning round going, Look what she did to me! Little savage!

My mother runs up quick and gets hold of my fists

and wraps them in her hands while Aunty Celia takes her hanky out and inspects Geraint's mouth. He's only bit his lip.

She's quite a firebrand, says Aunty Celia, pulling him ahead of us, You'll have to learn to be nicer, Geraint, if you two are going to live together.

Over my dead body, he says, but with a lisp this time, Thstinking Peathant!

I'm ready to have another go but my mother's got me in the Vulcan Nerve Pinch.

Hold that temper, my girl, she says out loud, but then she leans in close to my ear and whispers, Save it for when he least expects it, Enid. Then use your Special Power.

Which one? I say, because I have a few, and she looks at Aunty Celia and Geraint ahead of us and smiles sweetly at them. Then she looks down at me and points her finger to the tip of her tongue, and she says,

The most potent weapon in your armoury.

Five

Har nar brarn car. Reined and reined the rugged rork...

What are you doing? says my dad. He's standing in my bedroom doorway with his donkey jacket on and his hand holding his face up. I look at him in the dressing-table mirror using just my eyes. I can't turn round because Hans Christian Andersen will fall off my head and hit the floor and wake my mother up again.

I'm prarctising, pater, I say, For Brarmdead. They'll warnt me to talk porsh like them.

I've told you, Enid, you're going nowhere. Now put the book down and get your shoes on.

Are we going into town? I say, forgetting about the book, which goes whump on the lino.

Enid, will you shut that racket! my mother shouts, and my dad disappears from my bedroom and into their bedroom and closes the door.

I don't put my shoes on. I tiptoe across the landing and have a spy. It's necessary to be really quiet because even though my mother likes it when I Do a Recce, I'm not allowed to do it on her.

...and get her some new vests on your way back, she says, She knows which ones.

She's not going, Maria. That's an end to it.

We're not having all this again.

Jesus Christ! he says, louder, so I have to rush back into my room, and a second later he's saying, Enid, get a bloody move on will you? I'm in agony.

We don't go into town straight away because my dad has an emergency appointment with the dentist on account of his teeth giving him Pain Like no Man can Fathom. My mother has been poorly all week too. They can't eat anything, so I've had cheese and piccalilli sandwiches every night for tea and Frosties every morning which is my favourite breakfast. I have to suck and not crunch them because my father says the noise makes his face ache.

Our dentist is called Mr Hassan and his teeth are white as snow. My mother says he's a good advert for his business but my dad says he's not really because looking at his perfect gnashers makes *him* feel like a failure. We have to sit in the waiting room for a long time and my dad keeps saying Oh Oh like that, and sometimes you can hear someone else in another room going Ah. Ah. Ah! When that happens everyone in the waiting room goes very quiet and makes snake eyes at each other.

Will I have gas again? I ask my dad, because I had it last time I was there when I was six.

For the millionth time, Enid, no! he says, and the lady opposite smiles and goes,

At least she's not afraid. You've taught her well.

He hasn't taught me well because he's also terrified of Mr Hassan. That's why he's wearing his donkey jacket when it's boiling outside, because he's worried people will see him shaking. His knees are going even now, up and down millions of times a second.

Mr Hassan comes out and smiles his perfect teeth

and puts his hand on my head which makes me want to crawl under my dad's coat.

Hello, shy one, he says, and crouches down so I can see his teeth really close up. I've gone as far in to my dad's legs as I can without causing an upset like I did last time when I got under his chair.

It's me, says my dad, pointing a finger at his face. Mr Hassan doesn't move for a second so my dad does it again, an even bigger point, and the side of his face is all blown out like Popeye when he's eating his spinach.

Oh, yes, dear me, says Mr Hassan, This way, please.

Stay there, Enid, says my dad, pointing again but at the chair, and I'm fine to be left alone because now I can practise in peace. They've got a pile of old comics on the table and I find all the *Buntys* and look at the *Four Marys*. Raddy is always my favourite but I have to see how Simpy gets on now that I am going to win a scholarship like she did and go to Bramdead.

I'm picturing Bramdead like St Elmo's with secret passages and great larks in the dorm at night scoffing tuck when I get a funny feeling that I've forgotten something really important. I've got my bus ticket in my skirt pocket so it's not that. I'm looking around me at what it might be, but secretly. Once I went to school and it was only at playtime I found out I hadn't put my knickers on that morning. It didn't matter that no one else could tell, I was scared in case they made us do gym or if I was naughty and had to stand on the table like Robert Crumb is always being made to.

But this is another kind of funny feeling and then I know: it's because in my head Bramdead is round the corner where St Saviour's is, and every day I get to go home like normal and see my mother Slaving in the Kitchen or out the back lying in the deckchair to Catch the Rays. But if Bramdead is in Devon then I won't be able to do that because Devon's a thousand hundred miles away.

And Raddy is just a girl in a story, and even if she was real, she wouldn't be my friend, she'd probably be like Lord Snooty who is Geraint in my mind. I'd be sick in the Rover every day so Uncle Horace would be going, Don't do that, old girl, all the time.

Then Geraint would say, She's just a peathant, pater, thimply ignore her. They would probably make me be a slave like in Who is Sad Sally? and get me to clean the fires at the crack of dawn and fetch the water from the well before I'm allowed any breakfast.

I'm feeling very sorry for myself and trying not to cry when the lady opposite says, Don't worry, petal, he'll be fine.

Who? I say, thinking she must've heard my thoughts about Geraint.

Your daddy, she goes, and nods at the door, He's in safe hands there, love. So don't you worry.

I want to say, Okay, but *he's* not an abandoned orphan with a locket round her neck with her dead mother's face inside it, is he?

And that's what I'd forgotten all along, and now it comes back it goes up all over my skin like getting into the bath when it's too hot: my mother lying poorly at home in bed, which is why I'm going to be sent to Bramdead. She's poorly for real and it's not even a story.

★

My dad has had two fillings and an extraction, which means Mr Hassan has pulled his tooth out. He's got it in a piece of tissue in his pocket even though Mr Hassan didn't want to give it to him because of Hygiene. He's going to have it made on a chain round his neck like the Merican Indians. Also, he's had anaesthetic which is like gas but comes in a huge needle which Mr Hassan hides behind his back until the last second.

That's all he'll tell me because he's finding it difficult to talk proper and anyway he's far too busy singing and blowing kisses at all the ladies that get on the bus. I think he must be so happy because he isn't suffering Pain Like no Man can Fathom any more. When his buddy Errol gets on outside the Salvation Army stop, he says,

What's this Carlo-boy, drinking at lunchtime again, is it?

My dad shakes his head and says,

Wo, mae, I bee to the den-hith, av'n I?

He shows Errol the bloody tissue in his pocket with the most disgusting thing I have ever seen inside it. My dad's tooth is brown and black and about a foot long. It's like the dinosaur tooth they showed us on a film at school. I can't believe he's had that in his mouth. No wonder he's been in agony and holding his face up all the time.

Christ! says Errol, who must feel the same as me about it, That's one hell of a gnasher.

My dad nods at him and his eyes go huge in his head.

Too' im thew hourth, he goes, holding up two fingers, Thed I go' Methi-herranean heeth!

Errol gives me a little smile and shakes his head, and I shake mine back at him but only a tiny bit in case my dad sees and takes offence. He doesn't notice anyway because he's started singing again,

I wan' you-hoo-hoo, to thow me the way-yay,

at the top of his voice so the bus driver twists his head round and says,

Mate, if you don't shut up I'll show you the way and no mistake. Out on that street, alright?

Errol helps me get my dad back in the house and my mother comes down in her Negligee. It is white see-through and beautiful and makes her look like a ghost, nearly. When I think about her being a ghost it makes my heart go stiff so I say,

Dad's had a tooth out and it's massive!

But she says,

Not now, lovely. Sorry Errol – waving at her Negligee – I'm not very well today. What's happened?

Maria, Maria, I juth meth a girl name Maria!

That's my dad on a new song.

He's been to the dentist, says Errol, Three sheets to the wind n'all by the looks of him. Anyway, how are *you*, Maria? he says, sliding his arm up the doorframe right next to her, What's cooking in *your* kitchen?

My mother is very Curt with him. She is quite often Curt with people she thinks are Causing Offence, like the lady in the Post Office who Couldn't mind her own Business if she was Sitting on it.

My mother gives him one of her looks up and down and sees the state of his shirt and says,

So Jeanette's not forgiven you yet, then?

And Errol just smiles and says, I'll be making tracks, Maria, look after yourself, love, and she says, You too, and slams the door behind him.

Don't you let him in if he comes back, Enid, she goes, pointing her finger at me like it's all my fault, then she crosses to where my dad is sitting in the armchair and she kneels on the floor in front of him and tries to get his mouth open. She's saying, Let me see, Let me see, but he's batting at her with his hand all floppy and she gets in a rage and starts batting him back, only harder, and they look like the dishrag puppies in Gordon's pet stall. Any minute now they'll be biting each other's heads and rolling about.

Enid, go and get a glass of water for your father, she says, and while I'm out of the room I hear her say, Carlo, have you been drinking? Have you? Have you? You know what I said last time.

I can't reach the glasses on the high shelf so I put the water in a mug. When I pass it to her I think she's going to hold it up for him to take a drink of, but she just looks inside it and then throws it quick

– dash, like that – over his face and all over the chair and everything.

Don't you *ever* go drinking with my daughter in tow! she says, And *never* bring that cheating scumbag back here again! Do you hear me?

And she goes straight upstairs.

I don't know who to go to first but I just check that my dad hasn't drowned or anything because Miss Lintel at school said you can drown in an inch of water when we were on a school trip to Roath Park lake and Jackie nearly fell in off the side. He's smiling and starting to snore. There's a bit of pink spit at the corner of his mouth but when I get near to wipe it off his breath stinks so I decide it's probably best to leave it heal in its own good time, and go and check on my mother.

Six

Once upon a time in a little town in Wales, there lived a princess called Nettle.

Why isn't she called Enid like normal? I say, but my mother goes,

You asked for a story, Enid, so trap it and listen for once... and Nettle was a very sad little princess because even though she lived in the most beautiful forest, surrounded by other princesses with gorgeous faces and hair like Brigitte Bardot, she wasn't as pretty, and didn't have big showy flowers like all the rest of them.

I asked for a poem, I say, Not a stupid story. I'm too old for stories.

Are you too old for a smack n'all? This isn't just any old story, Enid. This is a parable.

Like the Good Samaritan, I go, Because we've already done that one at Sunday School.

Yes, but not that one. You haven't heard this one, okay? Now shut up. All day long Nettle was surrounded by these other princesses in the beautiful forest. There was Princess Anemone with her fabulous blue coat and frilly tiara, and Princess Hawthorn with her white wedding dress on, and Queen Anne in her lace gown, and they were all loved by everyone in the town, because people came from far and wide to walk in the beautiful forest and admire the loveliness and the tranquillity of it, and to eat in the local restaurant and drink in the pub and buy stuff from the gift shops on the high street.

The tourists weren't allowed to pick the wild flowers but some naughty ones did, they picked lots of different ones, but never little Nettle, no one ever picked her. And whenever the town people wanted some free flowers for their living room, like the farmer's wife or the carpenter's daughter, they always picked Buttercup or Meadowsweet, or any of the other flowers in the forest, but they never picked Nettle either.

People came from other towns and villages to pick Bluebell or Violet when no one was around to stop them, but they took one look at Nettle and went, Oh no, don't pick *her*.

I'm starting to feel a bit grumpy about Nettle never getting picked for anything. Fat Karen at school never gets picked for anything when we do games because she's fat, but she's really good at throwing and catching all the same so somebody really should pick her, especially for rounders. I want to point this out to my mother, but she's well into her story.

One day a new lady came into the forest. Her name was Lady Muck and she had come down from London with her husband Lord Muck, who had bought the manor and the forest and everything else. Lady Muck didn't know anything about plants or anything, and she saw little Nettle was wearing her best flowers, so after she picked Daisy and Marigold and Iris, she started to pick Nettle. Oh no, she cried, What's happened to me? And she ran away home to her husband Lord Muck, and told him how Nettle had attacked her and made her feel terrible pain all over.

What happened? I say, because now that Nettle is having a revenge I'm very interested.

Ssh. Anyway, Lord Muck was so cross, he ordered all his guardsmen to go into the forest and kill Nettle so that his Lady would never be injured again. And the men went with their huge scythes – yes, Enid, like the one the Grim Reaper's got – and they found Nettle and they chopped and chopped and chopped her right down to the ground. The people in the town all stood outside their houses because they could see the sunlight flashing off the guardsmen's blades and it looked like the sky was crying silvery tears, and they could hear the swish, swish as their scythes cut through poor Nettle's body and it sounded like the wind was wailing in sorrow. And all because one silly Lady from London thought it would be nice if she picked Nettle for her flower arrangement.

Is that the end? I say. My mother is looking at her hands in a very sad way, and I'm feeling very sad too and sorry for poor Nettle. Then she goes, Hang on, and shifts herself up the bed a bit.

Then night came, and the forest went dark, and all the animals started to come out of their homes. And when they saw the devastation and the terrible punishment inflicted on Nettle, they were horrified. The rabbit called an emergency general meeting and when all the animals were assembled in the fallen tree circle – the fox and the mole and the deer and the vole and the owl etc; he said, Look, Nettle used to hide my secret burrow and now the Poacher can see it! And the fox said, Me too! The dogs will find me easily. And the vole said, Me too! She always protected us from harm! Only the owl said nothing, because he could see that Nettle was no longer there to hide the field mouse, who he looked at with hungry eyes.

What shall we do? said the mole. Any ideas? said the rat, and then in one little corner of the forest a teeny tiny voice could be heard. It was a bee, late getting home.

I haven't been able to collect enough food for my children, it said, We will all starve! I suggest we go on strike.

And the motion was carried unanimously. Next day, the news spread. The butterflies went elsewhere for their groceries and the fox left his lair for a safer place and the owl had to go hunting over the hill because all the tiny animals had quit. And over time the lovely forest became an empty and ghostly place, with no birdsong and no butterflies or bees, and because there was no wildlife left, the following spring, there were no blossoms on the trees and no flowers in the field. And word got round that the forest was rubbish, there was nothing to see except the bare branches of the trees and empty cans all over the floor from when the local boys would have a session, so the tourists stopped coming and then the pub closed down and the restaurant became a charity shop and the gift shops started selling hamburgers and doughnuts to make a living. The end.

The end? Mam? What about Nettle's revenge? I say, because everyone knows you can't end a story just like that, especially not a parable anyway.

Oh. Okay. Then one day, the Lady heard about the Dead Forest as it was now known, and so she went to see for herself. And it was true, the forest was a very sad and barren place. Except in one far corner down a steep bank where the guardsmen couldn't reach, and there the Lady found Nettle, all on her own.

What have I done, the Lady said, Where are all the beautiful flowers and the birds and bees etc, and Nettle, who had had plenty of time to think about giving the Lady a piece of her mind, said: Lady Muck, do not dismiss the Nettle in the forest. I may not be the most beautiful flower, but I am not to be messed with. You hurt yourself once when you tried to take me, but I must stay here for a reason. You had no right to send the troops in like that. I will do you no harm if you just leave me alone and let me be of benefit to the rest of Mankind.

And the Lady made her promise, and allowed Nettle to spread herself out across the rest of the forest as far as she liked. And news got round that

Nettle had made it safe again and the birds and bees came back, and the flowers grew, and the rabbit and the vole and the field mouse etc, all felt a bit safer. And the tourists came back to the town, and everyone was happy again. Because everyone realised that Nettle was a smart cookie, and no one should ever mess with her. The end.

And the moral of the story is...? I ask, because that's what Major Windley always says at the end of his parables in Sunday School.

The moral is, if that Geraint starts to pick on you, you just tell him: he's got no right, and you will do him no harm if he simply leaves you alone.

And lets me be of benefit to Mankind.

Exactly.

But mam, what if he doesn't listen?

Then you punch his lights out.

Seven

Thurday 1st of july

Dear Mam and Dad

Everything here is ALL RIGHT. I was sick in the car on the way down and Uncle Horace swore when I did it again. It was only a Bl--dy but Aunty Celia said NOT in front of the child dear. It is very hot and Aunty Celia has bought me a new hat since yesterday I got sunburn by the pool. She calls it a bonnet and she put me some ~~camolile~~ ~~calollile~~ pink stuff on which made me go all white and she lets me have ice lollys when I want and choclate. My hat is made of straw and flowers round it like ann of green gables weres.

How are you? Do you like this picture? It is

of the beach ~~wear~~ where we will go on sunday if the wether is nice. Lots of love, Enid xxxxxxx

Saterday 3rd of july
Today we will go to see Gerant at the sports day. Aunty Celia has brought me a new skirt to go and it is stripes like your bathers only orange and yellow stripes. She says to say Hello and sends her best wises. It is HOT here!!!! Is it hot home as well? How are you? I ~~wh~~ hope you are feeling better and I am putting loads of kisses here for you xxxxxxxxx and here for dad xxxxxxxxx. Enid xxxx

Sunday 4th of july
Dear mam and dad how are you? spots day was very fun. All the boys did running but not like when we does the sack race or wheelbarrow Event. Gerant was winner in The fives which is like tennis only diffrent. Uncle Horace says today is Independance Day so I will draw you a picture of the Merican flag when we come back

from the beach. I got bit by a bee yesterday at the sportsday and Aunty Celia says that's lucky becase they only go for Gerant normally and maybe it was my skirt all stripey like a bee aswell? It is a big bump and quite sore and Aunty celia put some of that loton on it. How are you? Can you send me some letters please? Thank you! Lots of love, Enid xxxxxxx
Ps I miss you

Monday 5th of July
me and Aunty celia went to the post office in ~~Tivaton~~ Tivetorn today to buy more stamps becase she had a argument with a lady in the vilage shop becase I was doing a flicky on the windmills outside in a bucket to make them go and lady said don't touch you little tike and aunty Celia said don't be so rude to my girl and she has bought me some water wings for the when I play in the pool she says I can only swim a bit in the little end until I am bigger. I WAS NOT drowning. Can you tell her I must swim

in the big end mam? How are you? Has dad got his new teeth yet in the fornt? Is your belly better? Please write to me. Lots of love, Enid xxxxxx

Thurday 8th of july
thank you for my lovely presant. It is fab. Lady-birds are my best insect. Aunty celia says I am to young to were earings but I am going to were them in bed when she cant see. Uncle Horace is bringinging Gerant home from school today and I cant go with them because they going in The Motor. Mr lock who cleans the pool up is coming round and he has got a ~~mostash~~ mostach like dad and he has got a beerd and he has got a fat belly and. Can we have a padling pool when I come home? Please write to me. Lots and lots of LOVE, Enid xxxxxx

Sunday 11th july
uncle Horace says I should be a writer when I grows up as I am always writing to you! Gerant

says I can Not spell and he will teach me and I told him what you told to Miss Lintel that day when you said that spelling is for fashits and he goes How dare you! I am not a nasty! It was very funny see his face. Aunty celia says I can have a Fountin Pen for Christmas and some Basildon Bond which is paper. Can you tell her I would like a Jackie album as well and a dog? How are you? How is your

Please write to me, Lots and lots of love FOR EVER. Enid XXXXXXXXXXXX

Tuesday 13th july
Dear mam and dad
Aunty Celia says the post is stuck and that's why yor letters are not here. She says they may be stuck in the big office waiting to come and Gerant has got stung by netle! (Not ME!!!! a real one!) and he threw the ball in next doors garden and shows me the secet passage but he got stung by netles! I did not laugh at him. Aunty Celia give him some calilime loton like

I had. She says it is a Cure All. I said does uncle Horace put it on his nose becase it is really red and she goes ssh it's not nice to say things about people. Shall I get Aunty celia to send some calimile for your belly? How are you? Here are some kisses xxxxxxxxxxxxxxxxxxxx Enid

ps I have lost one earing but aunty celia said never mind it's the unlucky 13 and she will get me some more.

Wensday 14th july
Dear mam and Dad,
it is very hot again. Gerant says it is hot as venus. Which is the hotest planet. I said what about the sun and he said it is not a planet stupid and I said what is it then and he said a STAR. Tell him it is not a star mam becase a star only come out in the night. I think he is stupid.

Uncle hoarce has bought a new TV set which is like telly only bigger to be ready for the Olympics and I am only allowed to watch TV for ONE hours a day!!!! Hope you are feeling better and PLEASE don't forget to anser this letter. Lot and lots of love.

Your daugter Enid xxxxxxxxxxxxxxxxxxxxxx xxxxxxxx

Ps. Gerant is a spaz and a Nasty!! (Don't tell him I said!)

Ps. I miss you mam xxxxxxxxxxxxx please anser this letter.

Eight

I want to wear my stripy skirt and my Goin' Wishin' t-shirt but my dad says, Enid, just wear your school skirt and blouse, there's a love. And those new sandals your mam got you off the market.

He's going to wear a suit he borrowed off Errol. It's crimpled like all Errol's clothes because Jeanette still won't forgive him. My dad plugs the iron behind the sideboard and moves the telly over a bit to the end and irons the trousers on top of the sideboard and then goes Fucking hell! when he sees the varnish all stuck on the back of the leg. He puts the jacket on and says, Enid, what do I look like from the back? and I say, Really Brill! like that, so he won't worry about it. He has not had his tooth fixed, so people will probably look at that anyway and won't even notice the stuff on his trousers.

Uncle Horace didn't drive me back home in The Motor but made Geraint come with me on the train. Geraint knows everything about trains. My dad was waiting for me on the platform at Cardiff and when he saw me he ran up and gave me all massive kisses and a cuddle and he gave Geraint a fiver. Then Geraint went straight back to Devon again. He says he likes trains, it's the only way to travel.

Uncle Horace and Aunty Celia and Geraint will be arriving any minute. My dad keeps looking at his watch and under the nets at the front window and taking swigs out of the bottle. Then he's looking under the nets again and he says, Here we go, and I think it must be Uncle Horace in the Rover but it's not, it's another car, a long black one with a box inside it, all covered in flowers.

Nine

My dad and Uncle Horace go out the back to shout at each other in private because our house is packed with loads of people. Mrs Mickey must have come home from Australia especially because she's here having a sherry and looking very interested in our yucca plant. Errol is here too in all white clothes.

When my dad first saw him, he said, Mate, what the hell is all that about?

And Errol said, I have become a Disciple of Yogi Bhajan. Travel light, live light, spread the light.

And my dad said, Go spread yourself back home and show some respect, mun, put a flaming suit on.

Then Errol pointed at my dad and said, No offence, but you're wearing it.

Danny and Terence and Michael are here too.

Michael gives me a fiver and says, Don't tell your dad.

I Do a Recce and see he's not wearing his wedding ring but then I remember that there's no one to tell it to, so I go, Thank you, and put the money in the tin on the sideboard where my mother keeps the family allowance.

Aunty Celia brings me some orange squash from the table.

Why's dad and Uncle Horace shouting? I say, and she goes, Never you mind, sweetheart, they're not really, they're just having a grown-up discussion. Look what I've got.

And she opens her purse and takes out the earring my mother sent me that I lost down in Devon. I don't know why but I think they were bigger in Devon. The Ladybird in my hand looks like just a normal size one nearly.

You've still got the other one, have you? she asks, and I nod but I feel a terrible feeling, because I don't know where it's gone. Looking at the ladybird makes all the spit go from my mouth and it's hard to swallow.

Geraint comes over and sits on the chair next to us and says,

Mother, may I have a sandwich please?

Aunty Celia sees Mrs Mickey looking at her with a purse mouth and her face goes red and she says, Of course you can, Geraint. No need to ask permission, you silly boy!

Geraint's arms are too long for his suit and he is wearing a massive watch that says twenty past two o'clock.

What have you got there? he goes, pointing his finger at my earring.

It's my earring, I say.

I don't say, You silly boy, even though I want to. I show him my earring and he goes, Ah, a ladybird. Ladybird, ladybird, but then he stops because he can't remember what comes next.

Did you know that the ladybird is really a beetle? he says, but Aunty Celia goes, Not now, Geraint, so he mooches off to get a sandwich but then she calls him back straight away.

Geraint, she says, and he goes, Oh! Sorry, and says

to me, Enid, would you like a sandwich too?

I don't want a sandwich. I don't like fishy stuff in sandwiches, or at any time, only piccalilli and cheese or piccalilli on its own. I think I should go and ask my mother if she can make me a piccalilli one but then I remember and the horrible feeling rushes right into me again. It goes whoosh! like that. Like when I didn't drown in Uncle Horace's pool but I got over to the side and bit my front teeth really hard on the steps getting out, and after I banged my toe on the onyx ashtray and when the bee got me on sports day. It's like all those all piled up on my head.

My dad says it's okay to feel sad and cry, but when *he* does it he pretends it's not crying. Like in the mornings when his handkerchief is covered in snot, and he says, Hay fever, my love, what a bugger.

When I came off the train and saw my mother wasn't at home Slaving in the Kitchen, I asked my dad and he said, She's gone, lovely.

Has she gone to be on a cruise with Mrs Mickey? I said, and he went, No, my darling, she hasn't.

People tell you to do lots of things, but mostly they

say, You've got to mind your daddy now, haven't you, and be a big girl.

I will mind my dad all the time but he is the big one and he has got a beard too as well now on account of his Trembling Hand, so he looks like Bluto.

My dad can make me a piccalilli sandwich, he's made one before, so I go and look for him outside. He's standing by the Beast with Uncle Horace and they are both smoking fags and my dad has a pint of beer and Uncle Horace has something brown in a little glass. Probably his Single Malt which he must've smuggled from Devon.

Whenever Uncle Horace got home from his works, he'd go to the Drinks Cabinet and say, Who's been at my Single Malt again? Was it that useless son of ours?

Sometimes Aunty Celia would go, Don't be ridiculous, Horace, he's only fourteen, you must have drunk it yourself, but mostly she'd say, Not in front of the child, dear.

Aunty Celia would never own up and I couldn't say because it was Our Special Secret.

I run up behind my dad but Uncle Horace is in the middle of talking so I stop going to pull my dad's arm and wait because my mother says it's rude to interrupt. He's going,

...not even as if she's your responsibility, is it, Carlo, old boy, and my dad goes, Wanna Bet, OLD BOY? like that so I think he might punch Uncle Horace on his nose like he did some man at The Rev when Danny got chucked out the door and broke his arm. Then they both see me and go quiet.

Just give it some thought, says Uncle Horace, really quiet, For Celia as much as for the child.

Then my dad turns round and goes, What do you want, Kid?

Sometimes my dad calls me Chicken and sometimes he calls me Trouble, or Nuisance, or Spawn of Satan when he's messing at being angry. And he often calls me Enid, which is my name. The way he says Kid is like when he's telling Robert Crumb off for swinging on our gate.

Can I have a sandwich? I say, and he looks into the back door and says,

Enid, there are a thousand bloody sandwiches in there. Go and help yourself. God knows...

I don't say anything to that because his voice is all wavy like it is in the mornings. I remember I've still got the Ladybird earring in my hand so I'm putting it creepy-slowly into his suit pocket for safety. He must feel me doing it because he stops right in the middle of his speech and grips my hand really tight through his suit and squeezes it and squeezes it like he does with the flannel when he gives me a face-wash. It's like an angry feeling because I can feel him shaking, but it's not, because when I look up, his eyes are crying. His mouth is like a hole in a hedge because of his beard being so thick.

Uncle Horace goes, You poor man, I'm so very sorry, and he starts blowing a trumpet into his handkerchief. But then my dad stops squeezing my hand and snatches it out of his pocket and holds my arm up in the air so it looks like I'm pointing at Uncle Horace and he says, Okay, then, take her. That's what you bloody came for! Take her!

Ten

Erbin Manor
Autumn 1976

Again, says Geraint, Repeat after me: I promise I will not spy on my cousin Geraint.

I promise I will not spy on my cousin Geraint.

Upon pain of death.

Upon pain of death.

Good.

Good.

No, Enid, you don't repeat that bit.

No, Enid, you don't repeat that bit.

I only say it because I know it will make him raging.

No! Stop repeating now!

No! Stop repeating now!

I'm warning you!

I'm warning you!

I have to run down the hall as fast as possible

because I can see his hand going out for the clock next to his bed, and here it comes, there it goes, whizz bang straight past me and then Smash! into the banisters. He is not very good at throwing. If Fat Karen from school was throwing that clock she'd have had my eye out. So far Geraint has thrown:

A book

A shoe

A pencil case

A statue of Wellington on his horse

A teatowel

A clock

And he has missed me every time. The statue of Wellington was the best because it smashed into a million pieces and then Geraint went all white and said, Holy Crap! The Old Man is going to marmalise you! until I said, But Geraint, I never threw it, did I?

We stuck it together again with the glue he uses for his Skylab Model which he has been building since the Year Dot, and put it back on the mantel-piece with only a bit of the horse's hoof missing. Uncle Horace has eyes like radar, Geraint says, so when he came in from his works I pretended to faint like a lady in the old films and Uncle Horace was so busy making sure I wasn't sick on the sheepskin he didn't even notice.

Afterwards, Geraint said, You were brilliant, you should be an actress with that talent. He said it in a very sarky way so I could tell he didn't have a Reprogramme like my dad says Errol had which made him go all funny and be nice on top when underneath he is still That Cheating Scumbag. So while Uncle Horace was in his Study studying, I got out my felt pens and coloured the hoof in black and now it looks perfect, nearly.

I spy on Geraint a lot, mainly because it annoys him but also because he never lets me play with any of his stuff ever since I broke his Docking Platform which was only a bit of a cornflake packet bent in half anyway. Geraint says he wants to be an astronaut when he grows up, and that is why he is building the Skylab so he can Familiarise himself with the Technology. One time I said, And I want to be a spy when I grow up, and that is why I spy on you, to

Familiarise myself with the Technology. He said, Firstly, girls can't be spies, Secondly, you have to be able to speak Russian, and Thirdly...

But by the time he got to Thirdly I was very bored and couldn't stand him flicking his fingers out like that for one more second. Who needs their fingers to help them count to three anyway? I have decided that Geraint is annoying and also my Nemesis as well which is a really bad thing for a spy as it is their sworn enemy and a villain and all that is evil. Also he is a Liar which is another very bad thing.

Geraint says his Skylab is a Prototype Model which means that it is the very first ever built, but I have seen him copying from a picture in one of his comics, so that is a Lie.

I do not like lies, so when I promised Geraint I wouldn't spy on him any more, I had my fingers crossed behind my back. That makes it not a lie, but a Cree, which is Welsh for Not Really. Spies have to be very sneaky.

Apart from promising (not really) that I won't spy on him any more, there are the other rules which

Geraint calls his Lines of Demarcation. When he said it, I said, Are they lines like the ones Miss Lintel gives to Robert Crumb? 'I will not swing backwards on my chair. One hundred lines, please, Robert Crumb.' Geraint said, Don't be stupid, they are limits, like lines you don't ever cross.

He pretended to draw a line on the carpet near his bedroom door and said,

Look, this is a line you must not cross.

Where?

It's an imaginary line, I mean... invisible.

I put my toe over the line and skidded my foot along the carpet.

Doesn't hurt, I said, Are you sure you've done it properly?

It's a symbolic line, he said, and he sounded so smug, I got suspicious, so I didn't ask him what a symbolic was as it was clearly a trick, I just went, Oh, in that case – and slid my other foot over the line.

Then I had to scram really fast because he was going for a throw. He's got about a hundred other rules, like, I must never touch any of his stuff, I must never say hello to him if he is outside with his pals, I must never have the last bits out of the cornflake packet, I must never even LOOK at his bicycle. Once I said, These rules are so boring, they're always things I must not do, and he said, Here's a rule you *can* do: fuck off.

That is a really bad Swear and I almost told on him before I remembered rule 53 hundred: Never tell on him to his mum and dad.

I went away to ask Aunty Celia what a Line of Demarcation was. She was busy dusting the Drinks Cabinet and checking all the bottles were lined up nice and said, Go and ask your father.

Can I? I said, and then she looked at me a bit funny and said, I meant your Uncle Horace. Ask him when he gets home.

But I will ask my dad anyway. I write to him every day, nearly, and he writes back a lot when he has time. He says things like, I hope you're being a good girl, say hello to everybody from me, but mostly he tells me what is happening in the world. He calls it Newsflash!

Newsflash! Errol is going to live in a yurt (that's a big tent like Chipperfield's circus have got) in San Francisco (that's in America).

Newsflash! Mrs Mickey fell off her scooter and broke her ankle in four places. I do her shopping on Saturdays now and she has TONS of Pale Ale!

Newsflash! Robert Crumb's dad was cleaning the leaves off the front path and found a Gold Watch! That's what he told the copper, anyway (Ha!Ha!).

He always says goodbye like this: Sleep tight, my lovely girl, and don't forget to say a prayer for your Mammy. Don't be sad, your dad xxxxxxxxx

He never says when I can go back home. I expect the roof will take a long time to be fixed, because I've been here twenty-seven days already and he hasn't said anything about it in his letters. I will write a list of things to ask him about next time I send him a letter, and I will ask about the roof as well.

★

Sunday 12th September 2mp
Dear Dad,
Can I call you Pops? That is what Gerant calls his dad when he not caling him Papa or the Old Man. How are you? Tomorow I starting school it is in a old ~~builing~~ building with big windows like in the horor films and Aunty Celia has bought me the unform which all the girls were (there are no boys! Brill!) How is the roof? When can I come home?? How is danny and have you see errol again? How is mrs mickey? Have you still got a beerd?

Dad, what is a Line of Deemarkshon? Is it invisble like barb wire? Gerant says it is a simbolick, what is a simbolick? Can it hurt you if you touch it?

Has robert crumb ~~app~~ said sorry for the window? He is Accur! Gerant says that is like a dog, only even more. Can we have a dog when I come home?

LOTS OF LOVE!!!!!!!!! Xxxxxx yor Enid.

Ps have they fix the phone box? This is our number is case you lost it last time 0392 477439

Lots of love xxxxxxxxxxxxxxxxxxxxxxEnid

Eleven

We are learning songs for the Harvest Festival next week. My new teacher is called Mrs Reynolds and she is very strict and says things like, Now, Jennifer, what is eight nines? and then Jennifer has to say a number. When she did it on me, she said, Now, Enid, what is eight sevens? and I said Four and everyone started laughing and she said, Stop Laughing At Once, and everyone stopped laughing at once really fast. I didn't know it was my times table, because I know them all the way up off by heart. It was like a trick question, the way she said it. Spies have to learn things very quick, so I am on Red Alert and Stand By For Action!

In my class there is Jennifer Watson, Rose and Emily who are The Twins, Cynthia Asquith and

Carol Curtis, and Annette someone who has got to sit on her own near the door because of her impetigo. There are lots of other girls who sit behind me who I do not know. When Mrs Reynolds does the register she only calls out the last name. The first day, I thought she didn't call me and then she pointed at me and went, Pay Attention, Erbin. Enid Erbin! And I said, Is that me? And she said, Hands up if there is anyone else in this room called Enid Erbin, and Jennifer started laughing through her nose. I said, My name is Enid Bracchi, Miss. And she said, Not according to this register, Enid Erbin.

I shall ask my dad about it next time I write to him.

Harvest Festival in my new school is not like at Saint Saviour's, when my mother always sent me with a tin of beans for the poor. When I said to Aunty Celia that I had to bring something, she went, Oh heck, and started cooking stuff for the whole day. I had to carry a big bread shaped like a plait and not drop it, and I would have had the cake too only Uncle Horace came in from his works and had a massive slice out of it. That caused a Discussion between Aunty Celia and Uncle Horace. I spied on them by pretending my Sindy needed ballet practice on the landing and then I memorised it and then I wrote it down in code writing in my special top secret spy file:

Cel: It's lwys the sme with yu. I'm stck hr in this gd frskn plc ll on my own. I mt as wll be dd.

Hor: Gddmm yu wmn it ws only a pcc of cke! Try kping yr bk out of the bttle for fve mns and gt sme prspctiv.

Cel: You crul bstrd. Is it any wnder? Yud drv a sint to drnk!

Hor: A sint! Dn't mke me lgh.

Except that when I read it back, I couldn't understand it. I shall have to learn Russian very quick.

For the Harvest Festival we are singing 'We Plough the Fields and Scatter' and 'All Things Bright and Beautiful', and some other songs I don't know. In assembly Mr Lane who plays the piano said, Would anyone like to suggest a new hymn for us to sing at the Harvest Festival? and Cynthia Asquith put her hand up and said, Sir! 'I've got a Brand New

Combine Harvester', sir! It was so funny but when I joined in laughing with Jennifer and Emily and Rose they all looked at me, and Rose said, Poo, what's that bad smell?

Cynthia Asquith has got glasses with one of the windows covered in a plaster. Mrs Mickey sometimes has a plaster on her glasses when she falls off her scooter and breaks them but not over the glass bit. When I saw Cynthia at playtime, I said, Is the glass broken? and she said, No, I have a Lazy eye. I said, Are you resting it? And she said, No, it's this one, and pointed to the one without the plaster on it. I told her about Mrs Mickey's glasses and now we are best friends.

I'm going to ask Aunty Celia if Cynthia can come round to play after school and then I will get a ride home in her mother's sports car with the lid down. Cynthia's mother is Mrs Asquith and she is a Governor and a Doctor when she's not governing, and her car is pure white. She looks like Penelope Pitstop when she comes through the gates with her yellow hair all covered with a long scarf.

Even though Mr Lane pretended to be cross when Cynthia suggested a new hymn, it didn't last long because he was standing outside the gates when Mrs Asquith came at hometime. He does that nearly every day while he is pretending to look after the playground, and you can tell when she is coming up the drive because he pats his hair down over the baldy bit and shakes his keys up and down. Then he waves at her and sometimes she stops for a minute and has a talk with him.

I have to get the bus to school every day now after the first week. Aunty Celia drove me okay on Monday and Tuesday, but on Wednesday she was twenty minutes late picking me up, and on Thursday I waited and waited outside the gate until the Headmistress came along and said, Who are you, little girl? When I told her she said, Come along with me, and I sat in her office and she rang Aunty Celia but got no answer.

Then a Policeman arrived with Aunty Celia looking really upset with her make-up all over the place and they all went into another room without me and closed the door. I thought it must've been about my dad, and my heart was banging so hard I almost forgot I was a spy. But after a bit I went up sneaky to the glass in the door and listened and the Policeman was saying, Most unfortunate, but I am afraid this is not the first time.

Then I could hear Aunty Celia going, Oh, sob, like that, and then she went, Oh my god, if Horace finds out! What will I do?

The Headmistress has a quite deep voice and she said, Surely, Reginald, we can come to some arrangement on this occasion? The circumstances are very unusual. It's not as if she was actually on the road.

There was nothing for a minute except flick, flick, which I think must have been the Policeman going through his notebook and I was right because then the Policeman said, Well, I can issue a caution, I suppose. Mrs Erbin, I must warn you that being drunk in charge of a motor vehicle is a very serious offence and I will not be as lenient next time. The penalty for an offence can be up to three...

And Aunty Celia said, There won't be a next time,

Reginald – Officer. I absolutely promise.

And then I had to get back to my seat quick because I could hear their chairs scrape on the floor.

The Policeman gave us a lift back home in his car, and I was excited and said, Can you put the hooter on? And he said, No little girl, it is not a toy. Now please do not distract me while I am driving.

After a few minutes I was feeling a bit sick but I didn't want to distract him again so I tried to open the window.

You will find those windows are locked, little girl, he said, and Aunty Celia joined in, very bright now that she wasn't going to jail any more, saying, That's to stop the baddies jumping out, isn't it Reg – Officer?

He started going on about some Unsavoury Characters and I tried not to be sick but then it was too late and I had to walk the last bit home.

When I got there, Aunty Celia and the Policeman were out the front, looking into a bush and talking. I could see Aunty Celia's car stuck in the bush with the door hanging open. She was saying, Thank you, I really appreciate it, and then he got in it and put it back in its normal place on the drive so it looked the same as ever.

What shall we say happened to the rhododendron, Enid? she said when he had gone.

She was looking at the bush and pulling bits of twig out from the hole, which was really quite big.

Shall we blame it on the gypsies? I said, because whenever Mrs Mickey finds something gone, my dad always says, Those bloody gyppos were around again last night.

I'll have to have a think. This can be our secret adventure, Enid, can't it?

Does that mean I mustn't tell Uncle Horace?

That's right, you're a clever girl. And don't tell Geraint, either. Are you thirsty, sweetheart? I'm quite parched after our secret adventure.

So, now I get the bus. It's okay. I just have to watch out for The Twins because even though they say their father has got a Range Rover to drive them everywhere, they always get on the bus the next stop after me and make a big deal of sniffing and saying Poo all the time.

Twelve

For my birthday I get:

A big thick book called the *Pears Junior Encyclopaedia*

A pair of boots which go all the way up the leg like Dick Whittington was wearing in the Panto last Christmas

A riding hat

A recorder for playing in the school orchestra

A gun

It's not a real gun, only a pretend one, but it has a star on it like the Sheriff's in *Bonanza*, and Geraint has shown me how to load and fire the caps. The smell is lovely when they go off, but after I do one whole roll, Aunty Celia says, That's enough mayhem for one day, thank you, Enid, and puts the rest in her secret hiding place, which I know about on account of being a spy. It was Geraint's old gun from when he was little but I don't mind a bit. My mother always says it's the thought that counts.

I want to wait for the postman for my dad's card but Aunty Celia says Uncle Horace has to be in his works early and is taking me to school in the Rover as a special treat. Uncle Horace lets me sit in the front and he has covered all the seat and the floor with plastics. I feel a bit funny being on my own with Uncle Horace because even though I have been here for sixty-four days, he is always at his works or studying in his Study when he comes home so I do not really know him. He wears special gloves for driving, like the ones the murderers wear on telly, and he says, Would you like a sweetie, Enid? which makes me go on Red Alert.

No thank you, Uncle Horace, I say.

They'll stop you feeling sick, he says, Go on, help yourself.

He leans over me and goes in the glove cupboard

and fetches out a tin with all different fruits on the lid. I am double suspicious now because he is being so nice. Maybe they're poisoned sweets and he is going to kidnap me?

Can you pass me one? he goes, so I think they must be not poisoned because I could give him a poisoned one if I wanted to, so I get one out for him and then I have a red one which is strawberry. Then I have a yellow one which is lemon, and then I have another lemon one because they are lovely and sharp, and then I'm going back in the tin to try an orange one and he goes,

I think that's enough for now, Enid, don't you?

He said I could help myself but he wasn't really telling the truth. Geraint must get his lying off his dad. I keep the tin in my lap anyway because he'll forget about it in a minute and then I'll have the orange one.

How are you enjoying school? he says, because adults always ask you that when they don't know what else to talk about.

Mrs Reynolds says I have got a musical ear, I say,

and then I laugh because it's funny thinking of my ear playing the piano.

Ah, yes, your Aunty Celia mentioned something about that. Maybe you should join the village choir, Enid? Geraint has been with them for the past four years.

Maybe, I say, thinking, No Deal, Buster, it's bad enough seeing him after school. I help myself to the orange sweet, and just as I'm going for a crunch, something goes Clonk! in my mouth. The sweet must have a big hard bit inside. I try to crunch it but my mouth feels all wrong, like something's missing. Then the hard bit pops out of my mouth and falls in the tin. It's my front tooth!

Uncle Horace goes, Oh, Enid, don't spit the sweets back in, that's revolting! but I go, It's my tooth, Uncle Horace.

Only when I say it, it sounds like, 'It'th my thooth, Uncle Horath,' and that makes me think of my dad when he had his tooth out and my mother kneeling down in her Negligee like a beautiful ghost and lying on the bed making her fingers walk like a caterpillar over my eyebrows and telling me all about Nettle's Revenge, and I can't hear her voice anymore and I can't stop feeling the awful feeling filling up inside me like a million caps going off inside my heart.

Uncle Horace takes me back home and he says to Aunty Celia, It doesn't matter, it's half term next week anyway. I'll try his factory.

Then he goes straight in his Study and shuts the door. Aunty Celia looks a bit cross for a minute, and she bends down really close to my face and says, Let's see, Sweetheart.

But I don't want to show her. The hole in her neck has nearly gone, so it's not that. I don't want her to take my tooth. I am going to give it to my dad to put on his Merican Indian necklace when he has it made. She says, Would you like some lemonade? and goes to fetch it for me.

My Encyclopaedia is on the table with my gun and my recorder and my riding hat, and my boots are under the table. I don't feel like having a go on my recorder or my gun and anyway Uncle Horace comes out of his study and sits down next to me on the sofa and gives me a cuddle. Then he says, I've got a surprise for you, Enid.

Thank you, I say, but not very truthfully because I don't really feel like having a surprise today.

You'll see, he says, It'll be here tomorrow.

Then he gives me another cuddle and goes to talk to Aunty Celia in the kitchen. I can't be bothered to go and spy on them. The place where my tooth used to be feels big and empty.

Thirteen

My dad's beard is so long now it's like the one Father Time has got, only black. He's sitting on the sofa with his arms stretched right out across the back like he does at home, and he keeps looking at me like I'll go invisible if he stops. He'll grin at me with his front tooth gone and I'll grin back with mine gone too, and it's hysterical when we do it, we can't stop giggling.

He was on the front drive when me and Aunty Celia came back from the shops. First I thought, I'm having a dream, because I have a lot of dreams about my dad, and my mother especially, but then he put his arms out and said, Come here, Chicken, and gave me a massive cuddle, which NEVER happens in my dreams. While I was cuddling him back, he got hold of my hand and put it with his in his jacket pocket and said, Post! and pulled out my birthday card.

Sorry it's late, Enid, but I wanted to deliver it in person, he said, which made my Aunty Celia laugh really high and clap her hands together. When we went inside, he brought out a little oblong wrapped up from his other pocket and said, Happy Birthday, my girl – and because I was just looking at the paper, he went – Go on, silly, unwrap it.

The first thing I saw was a picture of my mother stuck on the front of a book. I knew the picture already, it was out of the Famous Family Album from when we all went to Tenby for our holiday. She is standing in the door of the caravan and smiling and her hair is down long and she has these shiny beads round her neck which she always used to wear and loads of bracelets going up her arm. She is the most beautiful lady in the world. The book is called: *The Water Nymph and the Dragonfly: Poems.*

Look inside, said my dad, and his eyes were nearly crying and Aunty Celia's eyes were nearly crying too.

The first page said, *For my darling daughter, Enid*, written in spirally black letters.

Did Mam write it? I said, because it didn't look like her handwriting.

Of course she did, said my dad, and then he saw my face and he went, It's her words, Enid, only when it's in a book they have to put it in print.

Like in the *South Wales Echo* when they do her poems? I said, just to be sure.

Exactly. She dedicated that book to you. And all of the poems are about you. Why don't you choose one and we'll read it together?

But Aunty Celia said, Shall we do that after lunch? Horace is leaving the office early today, so we can all eat together. I'll just go and call Geraint.

My dad gave her a look, but then he grinned at me and I grinned back and we were in fits again, and Aunty Celia said, I can't imagine what's so amusing.

She did a funny little dance like she needed a wee, which she always does when she gets her Nerves on, and then she went into the hall and shouted up the stairs, Geraint, get out of that stinking pit of yours! which is something she has never done before in Living History.

Geraint spends nearly every Saturday in his bedroom with the door shut, and all the nights when he isn't out doing sports or singing practice. At first I spied on him a lot, but I never heard anything, only sometimes he would go, Aah! Aah! Aaaaah! like that. The first time he did it, I pretended I was just passing on the way to the bathroom and knocked on the door and said, Geraint, have you got toothache? because it sounded a bit like when my dad was at the dentist. But he didn't say anything, everything just went dead quiet. The next day when I heard him again, I said louder, Geraint, have you still got toothache? And he opened the door all hot in the face and said, Fuck off you little squirt.

So I don't suppose it is toothache only something quite painful which he doesn't want to burden me with on account of me having no mother and only a father far away.

My dad has got a new tattoo; he shows it to me in the dining room while we're waiting for Uncle Horace to come. It is a big heart with an arrow going through it on his chest just on top of where his real heart is. It's got Maria written inside and flowers going in and out of the arrow and a gap underneath. When I touch it with my finger it feels all scabby.

I'll have Enid put in there next, he says, pointing at the empty bit.

When I'm dead? I say, and my Aunty Celia drops the knife in the sink.

Enid! she goes, Don't say such things!

It's all right, Ceel, goes my dad, It's a perfectly good question. Then he turns to me and says,

No, I'll get it done next week, when this part has healed. The two people I love most in the world.

Have you got any more? asks Geraint, and in a jiffy my dad has got his shirt off and is showing him:

The horse called Pegasus on his left shoulder
The Celtic cross on his left arm
The Eagle in Flight on his left arm
The Welsh Dragon on his right shoulder
The Italian flag going through the Heel of Italy on his right arm
The Chinese lady with the parasol in the middle of his back

The Pouncing Leopard on the bottom part of his back which always looks like it is jumping out of his trousers.

Geraint goes very white, and Aunty Celia goes really pink and says, My, Carlo, your work must keep you very fit.

Then she drops the knife in the sink again and pretends to be looking for it in the bubbles.

You'll do yourself a mischief, goes my dad, and he's laughing and swishing his hand in the water and she's going redder than a beetroot. Then the keys go in the front door and she runs out to the hall and the whole world can hear her going, Horace, darling, it's you! and Uncle Horace goes, Of course it's me, who else would it be? Have you had your beak in the trough again?

It's soup and smoked salmon for lunch which is fish and horrible, like eating a slimy sock, so I only have soup and bread and tomatoes with loads of salt on them. The adults are having one of their polite conversations which is very boring, so to amuse myself I play at annoying Geraint. The best way is to copy every single thing he does. He reaches for his spoon, I reach for my spoon. He picks up his butter knife, I pick up my butter knife. He butters his bread, sweep sweep, I butter mine, sweep sweep. He takes a slurp of soup, I take a slurp of soup. He sighs, I sigh, he sighs louder, I sigh louder. I can do this all day. But then he leans back in his chair really sneaky and lands me a massive kick under the table so that I can't help but go Ow!

Everyone stops talking and looks at me, but the rules mean I can't tell on him so I pretend I banged my elbow. My dad stares for ages at Geraint and in the end he says, What's the matter, Laddo?

Nothing, Sir, says Geraint.

So, you kick my daughter for nothing? Have I got that right?

And Geraint goes, She copies me, Sir, it's quite annoying.

My dad keeps staring at him for an awfully long time. Then he says, It's so annoying, is it, that you have to inflict violence on a small child? How old are you, son? Fourteen? I joined the merchant navy when I wasn't much older. I'll tell you what's annoying – and he leans right across the table and really close to Geraint's face so that his beard is nearly in his soup – Bullies. They get my back up something chronic.

It all goes very quiet and Aunty Celia takes a really big swig of her tonic water, and another one until it's all gone, and for the first time ever Geraint goes red.

Carlo, old chap, says Uncle Horace, You know what children are like...

Listen to me, says my dad, and he looks all round the table at us, I'm very glad you've offered to mind Enid while I get myself sorted out. But I won't have her bullied. Never in my lifetime. Has he hit you before, Enid?

I could say, he throws a lot of things and tells me to Fuck off nearly every day, but Geraint is giving me the Look of Death, so I go, No. He's just a pansy.

And then everyone is in hysterics. I don't know what a pansy is, except that Geraint calls Les and Woody pansies when they are on *Top of the Pops* because he really hates them.

I see she's picked up some interesting language while she's been here, n'all, says my dad, and Aunty Celia gets up and holds her glass in the air and goes, Little top-up, anyone?

★

If I hold on hard enough, he won't be able to go and he will miss his train.

Enid, my girl, he says, and he's pulling at my fingers, It won't be long now.

Every time he pulls off one finger I put another one back. I can last a long time doing this and he knows it.

As soon as the roof is fixed, you'll be able to come home.

Have they got the aeroplane out of it now? I ask, getting a grip with my other hand.

They have, darling, but the hole needs fixing yet.

Why can't I sleep in Mrs Mickey's shed with you? We could make me a bunk bed with some wood or

I could sleep in the deckchair.

I've told you, there's no room. And there's rats n'all. Can't have my only girl bitten by vermin, he says – and his eyes go daggers at Geraint – I'd have to twist their necks, wouldn't I? And that would upset the Vermin Authorities. You'll just have to be patient, my lovely. We'll be back together before Christmas, I promise.

Uncle Horace is giving him a lift to the station but I can't go on account of being sick, even though I wasn't sick last time when I ate the fruit sweets. We're all standing on the drive and Uncle Horace is swinging his keys round on his finger and looking very interested at the hole in the bush.

Hold on, mate, says my dad, and he gets my grip off his trouser leg and goes to the bush.

What happened here? he says, and Uncle Horace shakes his head.

Gypsies, apparently, he says, Trying to break in. Probably saw the Rover on the drive.

Not being funny like, says my dad, But why didn't they just come over the gate? Or walk through it?

Uncle Horace gives his keys a swing and says, Ready, old boy? and Aunty Celia runs out of the house with her legs all over the place and gives my dad a huge kiss on his face which he thinks is hysterical. I know because he's looking at me over her head and giving me the waggly eyebrows. She's going, Any time you'd like to visit, Carlo, you just – you just let me know. Any time – until Uncle Horace says, That's quite enough from the Farewell Party, Celia, if you don't mind. Why don't you go and have a little rest?

I wave and wave until the car is gone over the top of the hill and I stand around a bit more because I know Aunty Celia will be having a lie down, and that means Geraint will be in the house and on the Warpath.

Fourteen

Geraint's not in the kitchen or the front room so I suppose he must be in his bedroom having a groan. I'm looking for my mother's book but it's gone from the table. My recorder and my gun and the boots and the hat and the encyclopaedia are still there, so it's not Aunty Celia tidying them away like she always does with my stuff. I have my craze feeling coming over me, so I march up to Geraint's bedroom and I don't even wait to hear if he's having a groan, I just go straight in. He's lying on his bed and he's reading my mother's book. He looks at me over the top of it and does a little cough and he goes,

First day – that's the title, by the way.
Here, see how the child sleeps!

We must move silent to the stars
We must listen for the rising moon,
Blah blah blah, blah blah,
Her skin on mine will be a dawning – My Gord.

Then he does a funny thing with his mouth and he goes, it doesn't even rhyme! What a crock of crap! And he throws it right at me. I don't even duck, because I am totally crazed now. The corner gets me on my head but I don't feel it one bit because I am killing Geraint on his bed. I'm smashing his face with my fists and he's laughing for a second and then he's going Stop! Stop! But he's still laughing so I won't stop killing him. Then he gets both my arms and grabs them so I can't reach his face but I'll just kick him to pieces instead but he looks at me and he goes, Oh, shit!

Then I see all the blood all over everything where my head has burst.

Get this cleaned up at once!

Aunty Celia is standing in the doorway with her

hair a mess, and she looks deadly at us and Geraint says, Mum, I think Enid has cut herself, but she says, I don't give a bloody damn what Enid has done. Get this pigsty sorted, and she goes zigzag down the corridor and slams her door.

★

Geraint has got loads of posters on his wall, exactly like I've got on my wall at home only different. He hasn't got David or Woody or Les, he's got someone he says is called Iggy Pop and some people called The New York Dolls, and some ladies with their swimming costumes on, and some boys called The Sexy Pistols. He says they are the Antidote to Everything that's Wrong with this Society. But I think they look very rude and untidy with their tongues poking out.

After Aunty Celia went back to bed, Geraint ran in the bathroom and came back with a flannel and a bowl. I said, Not on your Nelly, No Deal, Buster! because I remembered last time when my toe caught on fire, but he said, It won't hurt, I promise. I checked his fingers weren't doing a Cree, and let him put the flannel on my head. It did hurt but not as much as my toe did so I didn't say anything, and then he took the flannel away again and said, It's bleeding like stink, hang on, and ran away this time into his mum and dad's bathroom.

I had a look in his mirror and he'd made a line down the middle of my head just below my hair which was very thin and very bleeding, especially when I waggled my eyebrows. I didn't know books could be a weapon and it gave me a brilliant idea. Then he came back with a stick like a lipstick only white-coloured and said, Right. Keep still, and he crayoned all down the cut bit.

Is it glue? I said, because I couldn't think what use it would be if it was just a lipstick, and he said, No, it's the Old Man's styptic pencil. Stops the bleeding. I hope.

Will I bleed forever? I said, and he said, Jolly well hope not.

Then he put a big square plaster on my head and

said, Don't do that stupid thing with your eyebrows, Enid, you'll make it start again.

When he went down to make me a cup of tea with five sugars for the shock, I had a really good spy on his room. It had got the posters and some books around and his desk with his radio on it and a stereogram and some records and a fountain pen in a case and his big watch on the table by the bed. But underneath the bed was the best thing ever, because it was absolutely disgusting with cups and plates and stuff with all green on them and socks and stinky underpants and right underneath there was a pile of naughty magazines like my dad's got with naked ladies on the front.

It was too late to get up when I heard Geraint and the saucer rattling so I fell myself sideways and pretended to have a faint.

Get up and drink this, he said, and sat himself on the end of the bed. While I was having my tea he went, Enid, what kind of aeroplane crashed into your house? all casual like, and I went, A massive one, of course.

And he went, What, like a 747?

Which was obviously a trick question because who has ever heard of that? I wasn't falling for it, so I just told him the true facts.

Actually, it was a Concorde.

What, you're saying Concorde flew into your house?

Correct, I said, because that's what Mrs Reynolds always says when I get my times table question right.

I didn't see it on the news, he said, and then he was quiet for a minute and let me drink my tea and then he said, And I didn't read it in the papers either.

It was in the *South Wales Echo*, I said, My dad told me.

Do you believe everything your father tells you?

Why shouldn't I?

This was clearly a trap and I was instantly on Red Alert and Stand By for Action.

Just wondering, he said, then he looked up at the wall behind him and went, Shall we get this off?

When I looked up there were millions of red dots all over the wall which were blood dots from when my head spurted. I rubbed one off with my finger and Geraint pulled a face.

Uggh, that's so unhygienic!

I didn't say anything, I just bent down by the side of the bed and got out his stinky underpants and then I said, Shall I use these, then?

And for the second time in Living History, Geraint went bright red.

Fifteen

Uncle Horace's Study is the brownest room I have ever seen. Every single thing is done in brown apart from the light on his table which is green. Uncle Horace is brown as well because he has on the brown jumper Aunty Celia's sister gave him for his birthday which is not until next month. When he opened the parcel, he went, O joy, and he must love it a lot because he wears it all the time when he is doing the garden.

He is sitting behind his table talking on the phone and writing things down on a paper with his fountain pen and apart from his red nose he could be the Invisible Man. I'm wondering if this room is like my dad's Brown Dudgeon. I'm not surprised he has to get pills from the doctor if it's brown like this inside his head.

I have to wait while Uncle Horace talks to someone about mines. I know they have mines in Russia, because I borrowed a book out of the library to help me learn Russian and be a spy, so I'm thinking he might be sending me to the coal mines so I must be in Serious Trouble. That is why I am here in the brown room.

After Geraint bust my head open with my mother's poems, I had this brilliant idea that I could use the *Pears Encyclopaedia* for spying. It was a very boring book anyway, so while Aunty Celia was having a lie down I got a pen out of the Secretaire in the hall which is just a dear sideboard, and put my gun on the top page of the Encyclopaedia and traced all round it like we did with our hands once at St Saviour's. Then I got the pointiest knife out of the kitchen drawer and cut all round where I traced. It took ages but it was worth it because after I cut out all the pages I had a secret place to hide my gun, which is called A Concealment Device which all spies must have for their weapons and secret files. But I ended up with loads of pages shaped like a gun that

I had to get rid of because as a spy you have to Destroy The Evidence.

I put the pages on the bonfire in the garden that Uncle Horace likes to do in his jumper, because that is Destroying The Evidence. But at teatime Uncle Horace came in holding a bit of paper that looked like a gun shape and said, What the devil might this be?

I didn't tell, because spies don't ever spill the beans even when they are tortured. But he must have bugged me with a special microphone because here I am waiting to Discover my Fate. Even though I didn't tell anyone except now I think of it I might have told my mother when I was saying my prayers last night.

He comes off the phone and goes, Sorry, Enid. Now, come here, and makes his finger in a little crook. I go round the table but not very near in case he is going to stab me with the fountain pen which often have poison inside them and are one of the best ways of killing a spy.

Let me look at you, he says, and turns the green

light round and points it in my face. He is going to interrogate me!

I will never spill the beans! I say, and he does a big laugh like a hoot and then he goes, It's alright, Enid, I think we both know who's responsible for this, and as he's saying it he's staring at the plaster on my head which is nearly falling off because I haven't had a new one since yesterday when it happened. He has a brown drink on his desk and he gulps it like medicine and says, We'll just wait for your Aunty, dear, and get to the bottom of it, shall we?

Then he goes in his desk and he puts the glass in the drawer and gets out a little shiny tin and he says, Want one of these? and inside the tin are white pills. They are just like the ones spies have to take when they need to die, so I say, No thank you, Uncle Horace. But then he puts a pill in his own mouth and I'm sorry I didn't have one because they're only mints and I love mints.

How did you get that cut, Enid, he says, all casual, and I say, all casual back, Oh, just a book just fell on me.

A book? You mean – let's use an example – the *Pears Encyclopaedia* that Aunty Celia bought you?

Umm, no, my mother's book of poems, I say, because his eyes are twinkling at me. I think he must be On To Me and the interrogation about the gun will start any minute now.

That's not a very heavy book, Enid, he says.

I don't really know what he means so I say, No, but the corners are really sharp.

At that second he has to stop his interrogation because Aunty Celia comes in and her hair is a fright like a nest all over her head, and she says, You rang, m'lud? in a very sulky voice. I'm wondering if she might be a Double Agent.

Look at the child, he goes, and she looks at me all down to my socks and then she looks back at him with the same face.

Notice anything different about her? he goes, which makes me Stand By For Action because *I* haven't noticed anything different about me and I'm me.

Look at her head, at her head, you appalling lush!

She's got a bloody great cut on it! That useless waste of space has gone and injured her!

What? Not the pool man? says Aunty Celia, He didn't let her fall in again?

No! Not Mr Lock, you loon! Our lazy good-for-nothing son!

Uncle Horace's face goes the same colour as his nose, nearly, and Aunty Celia has a tizzy and puts her hands up to her cheeks and says, Oh, no, I'm such a bad mother. Whatever happened? What did he do, darling?

So I start to say, You know when – and I'm going to say – when Geraint hit me with the book yesterday and you shouted at us to clean up the pigsty, but instead I don't say anything. My mother told me my tongue is The Most Potent Weapon in my armoury but you must only use your most potent weapon when you've got no other weapons left and I have still got my gun. And anyway my tongue doesn't want to be a weapon against Geraint, even if he is a Useless Waste of Space and a Good For Nothing.

What shall we do, Horace? she goes, and he flops

back in his seat and has a long think and says, Enid, can you wait outside please? We won't be a minute.

I am really happy to wait outside because it is easier to spy on people when they aren't watching you. I leave the door open a little crack so that I don't have to bend down to the keyhole because bending makes my head go bang bang like that on the cut bit, and I hear Uncle Horace with his strict voice on going,

Firstly, you will take her to Doctor Phipps and get that wound checked out this morning. She'll probably need a tetanus jab. Secondly, you will drive her there and you will drive her back and there will be no incidents of the gypsy variety. And thirdly, you will keep your nib out of the Quink and look after this child properly until we have to give her back to that orang-utan she calls her father. Have I made myself clear?

What about Geraint? says Aunty Celia, I told you he needs help with his problems, but would you listen, would you?

I will *help* Geraint with his *problems*, he says, Leave that to me.

Then it goes quiet so I run quick over to the Secretaire and pretend to be admiring the shininess of the top bit and Aunty Celia comes out putting her hanky up her sleeve and says, Get your coat, sweetheart, it looks like rain again.

The interrogation must be over and They Know Nothing! If I say so myself, I am becoming a very professional spy.

★

Will I have a scar?

Nope, don't think so.

The doctor is putting really thin bits of string all the way over my cut one by one without even using a needle and cotton.

I'm a bit sorry I won't have a scar, partly because all the best spies have them, but mainly because every time I saw it, it would let me think about my mother's book and then I could think about my mother as well.

I have read all of her poems now as they are very

little and easy. Geraint is right though, they don't rhyme, but that's probably because my mother was very busy Slaving in the Kitchen all the time and couldn't think of the words to rhyme with the other words.

The one I like best is about the nymph who lives under the water like Aqua Marina. One day she goes, Bye bye, see you later, to all her nymph friends and climbs a ladder up to the sky but she never comes back down because when she gets to the top she grows big wings and they keep making her float and won't let her go down again. It sounds sad but my mother says in the poem, Now she dances on the water, or something like that, and I think my mother means she is probably in Australia on a cruise like Mrs Mickey was before she came back and broke her ankle in four places.

Sixteen

Don't sulk, Geraint, you're not a baby.

Nor is she, he goes, and prods his pointy finger right in the back of my head, It's not fair!

Life's not fair, says Aunty Celia, It's about time you learnt that. *You* used to get car sick when you were little.

So?

And we let you sit in the front, don't you remember?

No.

Geraint is very cross because every time Aunty Celia takes us to choir practice he has to sit in the back seat and I must sit in the front because the front is where I do not get sick. I have been going to choir practice for three times now, and the teacher is not a teacher he is a Vicar. You would never guess though because he doesn't have a Vicar dress, he has on jeans and just an ordinary shirt and wears his hairstyle like a Young Person. He likes Young People, they are The New Blood of Christ, and he also likes to be called by his ordinary name which is Alexander, but not all of it.

Call me Zander, he says, whenever anyone forgets.

Vicar goes, Ah, the New Blood! when he sees me and he smiles like he's lost a penny and found a pound. Then sometimes he says to Geraint, Don't sing this bit, Gerry, there's a good chap, on account of Geraint's voice going up and down a lot and making us sound like a Nest of Badgers.

We sing 'O Come All ye Faithful' and 'Silent Night' and 'Away in A Manger' and 'We Three Kings'. I know all the songs off by heart but even though Geraint has been going to choir for years, he always forgets the words. He goes: *While shepherds washed their cocks by night*, or he'll sing, *On the first day of Christmas my true love gave to me, A suck job in a pear tree*, which always makes the boy behind him laugh.

The boy behind is called Jeffrey and he has got a

million pimples all over his face covered in pus and his breath is really, really bad as well so I try to stand on the other side so he is not putting his dragon breath all over my head when he's singing and making my hair go green. The lady behind me is called Mrs Price-Porter but everyone calls her Mrs PeePee which is hysterical. She has got the asthma really bad and sometimes she takes out a little tube between the verses and makes a noise like a fart.

Vicar likes me to sing a bit on my own, he calls it the Solo. I think it is because he must know I can speak Russian and am brilliant at foreign languages.

This is you, Enid, he says, when it comes to the bit where I have to go,

Glor-or-or-or-or-or, Glor-or-or-or-or-or, Glor-or-or-or-or-or-or-Ria! Hosanna in Exchelsiss!

It is my favourite part of the whole song.

We are in Final Rehearsals for the Christmas Concert next week, even though actually Christmas doesn't start until the week after when I stop going to school and go home to my dad.

I'm pretending that I will be still stuck here because

it is Peace and Goodwill all round the Land with Geraint not allowed to be so Waste of Space and Uncle Horace being funny and Aunty Celia not Mainlining the Malt, as Geraint always calls it when she's dusting the drinks cabinet, which means her hair looks much better.

Aunty Celia gets very excited about Christmas. She says this time of year is Thrilling. At dinnertime, which happens at night in Devon, I ask her if she wants anything from Santa, and she stares all funny at Uncle Horace over her cola and says, Um, let me think. A new car? And then I ask Uncle Horace and he says, Um, let me think. A new wife? which makes Aunty Celia look very cross, so I go quick to Geraint, What do you want? and he gives a little speech like this: Christmas is just a bourgeois institution designed by the Powers That Be to fool the lumpen proletariat into spending their hard-earned money on unessential frippery. It is what Marx calls the opium of the people.

Uncle Horace does one of his hoot laughs and says, Then you won't be wanting that new Casio that you're always harping on about. Excellent. I shall save my hard-earned money. By the way, I think you'll find he was referring to religion.

Splitting hairs, old man, says Geraint, but he looks cheesed-off all the same and starts chopping his gravy into blobs.

And what about you, Enid? says Aunty Celia, Can you guess what Santa's going to bring you?

I have a little think. It probably wouldn't be a dog. It probably wouldn't be a Bionic Woman doll even though I would love that, she has got a bionic ear which must be really good for spying. What I would like is for Santa to fly me home on his sleigh so I could be with my dad. But before I can say anything, Aunty Celia says,

I'll give you a clue. What is your hat for?

My head?

Your riding hat?

My riding head?

You're getting warm, sweetheart. How would you like a pony?

I'm going to tell her I'd much prefer to go home

when Uncle Horace starts choking on his dinner and we all rush round to hit him on the back and fetch him some water. When he has stopped crying he says,

Celia, can we have a word in private? and they go off to his Study. I can't go and spy on them because Geraint is still sitting smashing his potato into gloops. He looks at me all sneaky and then he goes,

You know the dress rehearsal for the Carol concert next week? and I go, Ye-es, in a way that means, Of course I do I am not stupid, and he goes, You know we're going on a coach? And I go, Ye-es, again, because it's all been arranged – Aunty Celia must take us to the bus stop in Tiverton and the coach will pick us up on the way to the Cathedral and then Aunty Celia will fetch us from the bus stop after we've done our singing practice.

What if the coach goes somewhere else? he says, and I've got no answer to that, because why would the coach want to go somewhere else? But he's carrying on, and as he's carrying on, I get a funny feeling he is making a plot.

What if the coach was going to Caerphilly?

The way he says Caerphilly makes it sound wrong, but then he goes, You do know where Caerphilly is, don't you?

Of course I do, I say, but it still doesn't sound like the Caerphilly I know which is in Wales. I don't tell him he's saying it wrong because he's well into his plot and doing his sneaky face which puts me nearly on Red Alert.

What if we went on a demonstration? he goes, Because Zander has got it all worked out.

But what about the concert? I say, because we have got to do the dress rehearsal so that we know where to sit and stand and everything.

Oh, he says, in a very haughty way, We shall be going to a concert, alright, Enid, don't you worry about that.

And then he points at my head where there's a still a scab because it's nice to pick it and he says, We don't want any more accidents, do we, dear cousin?

I am totally on Red Alert now, but even before I can get my fingers in a Cree, the next thing he does is makes me Swear, On Pain of Death, not to tell Aunty Celia or Uncle Horace anything about Zander's plan.

★

So, Enid, are you looking forward to the dress rehearsal? says Aunty Celia, all casual. I'm sitting in the front of the car on all the plastics and Geraint's right behind me with his knocky knees bumping the back of the seat, so I don't say anything, I just nod.

What about you, Geraint? In good voice? she goes, Ready for *action*?

Yuhh, he says, which means Yes in normal words.

Even though I haven't told a lie or anything, I'm keeping my fingers in the Cree position just in case I have to in a minute. But Aunty Celia doesn't say anything else except, What horrendous traffic! Christmas shopping! every ten seconds until we are nearly at the bus stop. The coach is already there waiting and Geraint starts getting all huffy in the back and says, Hurry up, will you! It'll go without us! Then he's belting out of the car before I can even get my door handle undone.

Aunty Celia does a little laugh and says, Hang on, Enid, I've got something for you, and she gives me her leather gloves out of her pocket.

It'll be cold tonight, she says, looking at me funny, You might need them.

In Caerphilly? I say, before I even think about not saying it.

Exactly, she says, and at first I think her eye is going a bit squinty but then I see she's winking at me.

You stay close to the others, dear, won't you? Don't go wandering off on your own.

She's doing her eye again so I think she must be On To Us about Zander's plot. I do what all the best spies do and Throw her off the Scent by showing her how I can bend the fingers of her gloves over backwards on account of them being too long for my hands.

Better get going, sweetheart, she says, and she leans over and gives me a kiss right on my head near the scabby bit. I think she must be quite brave to do that because I don't even like *looking* at her neck even though the hole is gone because it makes me feel like the floor is jumping up at me, and I wouldn't kiss it for a million pounds. Then she goes, Yakki Da, Enid, and does a funny laugh.

I don't know what to say to that. I think it must be Russian and that she is letting me know that she is a spy as well, so I wave at her with my extra long fingers to let her know I have Deciphered her Code.

Seventeen

There are twelve of us going on the coach not counting Mrs PeePee's dog who is a Yorkshire Terrier called Nancy after Nancy in the Oliver film.

Vicar jumps on first and sits right at the front near the driver where he can speak loud at everybody if he wants to. I would like to sit in the front too because I don't know if I will be sick on the coach but I probably will be sick, but before I can get on some old people push in front of me and one says, Age before beauty, and another one goes, Mind your manners, little girl.

I don't say, It's rude manners to push in, because Uncle Horace says that in Russia they have queues everywhere all the time, so I must get used to it and not get my craze on if I am going to be a Secret Agent Undercover.

Geraint and Jeffrey are behind me and Jeffrey is whispering in Geraint's ear. I don't know how he can stand it, I get whiffs of his breath from miles away. Then two girls get on and Jeffrey and Geraint start whistling the Muppets song, then they go quiet and beetroot all of a sudden because Serena is coming as well. Serena is the most perfect girl ever and when she comes to choir practice Geraint starts doing a funny thing with his neck, like he's trying to stop his head from falling off, and sometimes he puts his hand in his trouser pocket and searches for his handkerchief. He can't do that today because he has got on new trousers which are very shiny and tight, so he just pretends to bend down and pull his sock up.

I've kept you a seat, Serena! goes Vicar, and she goes, Oh, sure, Zander, like she couldn't care less and swishes her skirt round and falls herself in the seat like she is very exhausted.

Mrs PeePee says, Come and sit with me, Edith, so I pretend I don't know who she's talking to because she always gets my name wrong and calls me Effie or Etty or something. But I would like to play with Nancy so I get on and sit next to her behind Serena. I Do a Recce on Serena because I have never been this close up to her before. I can only see a couple of bits, like her arm hanging over the end of the seat which has got bangles going all up it like my mother used to have and golden bits in her hair. She smells really lovely. She smells like my mother.

Geraint and Jeffrey go right to the back of the coach really quick and then we're off. Vicar gets up as we're going round the roundabout but the driver says, Sit down, Mate, so he sits down again. But he gets up again when we are going in a straight line and says,

Welcome everybody, I'd just like to say a few words before we hit the motorway. Now, we all know why we're here today, but before we say a prayer and ask the Lord for courage and fortitude, we must take this opportunity to remind ourselves that we are soon to witness the most massive degeneration and rampant evil that the world has ever seen.

It is vital that we present a unified front against Satan and all his minions and show how the power of Christ can destroy unclean and dare I say, lewd, thoughts and habits of these lost souls through hope and righteous judgement...

Vicar can be very boring when he drones on. Anyway, I already know everything, because Geraint has told me and I have kept it secret on Pain of Death, even though Aunty Celia knows all about it. She would make a brilliant secret agent if she ever gets fed up of being a lady. We are going to demonstrate against the Evil Force that is appearing in Caerphilly tonight. We are going to sing our carols outside the cinema to stop Satan and his Sexy Pistol gang from Wreaking Havoc and Destroying the World as We Know it.

When Geraint said we were going to the cinema I got quite excited because I love going to the pictures, but he said, It's not a film, stupid, and *you* won't be going in, then he did his little laugh which just showed his top teeth and looked very sneaky. I must be on Red Alert when he does his laugh, because it means he will pinch me or ping my ear when nobody's looking.

I get up and turn round to see if he has come up behind me, but he is still at the back with Jeffrey. They are pulling faces out of the window and sticking their fingers up so I sit down again and Mrs PeePee says, Would you like to have Nancy for a bit, Elsie?

Nancy is very small and trembly. When I put her on my lap she starts going round and round on my skirt and twisting it up all creased, then she huffs down right in the middle. I try to pull my skirt out a bit but she starts doing this growl. It starts off small but gets bigger and longer until Mrs PeePee says, Oh, I think she likes you, Edna.

I can't move very much for a very long time so I look at Mrs PeePee to take her dog back but she is asleep with her mouth open. If I even go to scratch my nose Nancy growls at me, so I shut my eyes and try not to think about being on the coach because that makes me think about being sick. I can smell Serena's perfume so I think about what colour it is to take my mind off being sick, and I decide it's not just one colour, it's like my mother's eyes, which are blue with green speckles in. I'm just picturing my mother's eyes and having a lovely dream when I hear Vicar going,

...special person in one's life, do you know what I mean?

And Serena going,

Yeah, Zander, absolutely.

So, you know, if you ever feel you need to talk to someone, I am there for you, says Vicar, and she goes,

Yeah, cheers.

And he goes, Because I completely understand that sometimes a young person needs a role model, someone who is absolutely trustworthy and will empathise with their situation and not judge them.

And she goes, Sure, that's good.

So, y'know, I'm here for you. That's all I'm saying.

Great, she goes, Thanks.

Because you must feel... I don't know, you must feel a terrible burden on you at this time in your life. I'm not so old, haw-haw, that I don't remember the lure of ascendant sexuality, the uncontrollable surges of desire.

And she goes, No, it's cool, really.

Because, you know, you must be, er, fifteen? Sixteen?

I'm seventeen, actually, she goes.

Then it's quiet for a bit and then he goes,

So, what are you doing afterwards?

Eighteen

I have never seen a boy look so stupid as Geraint looks in that get-up. If he thinks Serena will fall in love with him looking like that he's got another think coming.

When we got there a million hours later and it was dark, Vicar asked the coach driver to drop us in the car park round the back of the cinema. Then when we were all off and I was being sick on the pavement he said, Right troops, rally round, I have something for all of you.

He went under the coach in the bit where they put the suitcases and he brought out a big box full of cardboards on sticks. The cardboards had writing on them, like, God is Not Your Enemy, and, Praise the Lord and Shame the Devil, and, You're Going to

Hell!!! and more stuff like that, and he wanted us all to have one to wave at the Sinners. The old people said, I can't hold that with my angina, and, I can't hold that with my walking stick, but the Muppet girls took two each and Mrs PeePee said, I will have one if Esme looks after Nancy for me.

She meant me, but it was No Deal, Gringo, because Nancy had already bit me twice on the coach, once when I tried to move my leg a tiny bit because it had pins and needles and another time when I was yawning. I have gone off dogs For Life thanks to her.

Geraint was being very kind all of a sudden which was really suspicious. He said, Hey, Zander, I'm just going to take Enid to the toilets over there so she can wash the sick off, we'll catch you up, and Mrs PeePee went – Who's Enid? I've got a cousin called Enid – but Geraint was pulling me over to the toilets in the far bit of the car park.

I went in and had a wash but not much because the soap was absolutely filthy and there was no paper and then I waited for Geraint and Jeffrey outside and they took for ages.

When they came out again they had done something horrible to their hair, which was sticking up all over the place even worse than Aunty Celia's after a lie down, and Geraint was wearing a collar round his neck with pointy pieces all over it and the toilet chain from the bathroom which went missing last night. It was hanging off his trousers.

Geraint, you found the chain! I said, because Aunty Celia would be quite delighted, and he said, Shut up, what do you know?

I didn't mind him saying that because spies always have to pretend they don't know anything, so I must have been doing a brilliant job.

Go and find the other nutters, he said, And remember what I told you – keep that buttoned.

I only noticed when he pointed to his mouth that he had a big safety pin in the side of his face, and then I saw that Jeffrey had one as well in the same place but his kept falling on the floor.

Why have you done that? I said, You'll have to have a tetanus now, and Geraint started talking but had to take it out to tell me off, so I could see it didn't go all the way through.

I pretended to look for the others but I was really going to spy on Geraint, so I hid behind the toilets until they went round the corner and then I tippy-toed after them. Only, when I got to the front of the cinema I couldn't find them because it was packed with boys and some girls and they all looked the same as Geraint and Jeffrey with their hair a mess and filthy clothes, like they had been in a terrible fight at school and got their tops ripped and covered in felt pen.

I thought I might be able to use the special power in my nose to smell Jeffrey's breath but there were quite a lot of boys standing about with facefuls of pimples and B.O.

After a while I got a bit worried because some of the boys were going, Who's this then? and, She's started young, and, Someone's lost their mammy, which made me feel quite suspicious, because how could they know that? Then a boy bumped into me and someone else pushed me in the side and I thought I might go Undercover and give up spying for a while and find everyone else because they would want me to sing the Solo part quite soon.

Then I had the brilliant idea that it would be really easy to find them because they would be holding the cardboards and singing, except there were millions of people singing and holding cardboards and most of them looked like the Muppet girls or the old people.

I thought I could go back to the coach and have a sit on it until they all came back, but there were loads of coaches in the car park and I couldn't remember which one was ours. I was getting a bit of a dizzy feeling in my head and my foot was hurting where someone had stood on it and my hands were cold because I couldn't remember what I'd done with Aunty Celia's gloves, but then I saw my mother standing by the side door with a man. She was smoking a fag and twizzling her hair around, and I ran up to her as fast as I could and put my arms round her middle and smelt her smell.

Hey, little one, she said.

And then I saw it wasn't my mother, it was Serena,

and a big bit of sick came up and stuck in my throat and made my eyes hurt and I couldn't swallow it. It was like when you swallow a bubblegum by accident and you can't make it go down, you just have to wait and it takes ages.

Don't cry, honey, she said, and she bent down and gave me a cuddle.

Not yours, I hope, said the man, who had a face like all the other boys, only a lot older.

She's a friend, she said, Aren't you? A very special friend.

Then she waved goodbye to the man and got me by the hand and as we were walking away, he shouted, Dosvidanya, beautiful!

And she said, Bye, Mal, see you again sometime.

What did he say? I said, when we were crossing the road.

Who? Malcolm? she went, Oh, that's just Russian. He likes to think he's *so* individual. Pathetic.

I don't know who Malcolm is but I'm glad that Serena knows Russian. Maybe she can teach me some. Maybe she's even a spy.

Nineteen

Cynthia Asquith and her mother have just arrived outside the church in their sports car. I'll have to find Serena really quick because I want to stand next to her in the choir and show Cynthia I have got a new best friend and couldn't care less.

I was very fed up when we got there and I saw it was just an ordinary church, because I had wrote a letter to my dad and told him we were singing in the Cathedral. If we had gone for our proper dress rehearsal instead of to the Demonstration I would have been Fully Briefed, which is good for a spy to be as it means they know everything. I'm worrying in case my dad takes the day off of fixing the roof and goes to the Cathedral and sees we're not there. Then he might go to the house instead but there'll be nobody at home because Uncle Horace and Aunty Celia have come to watch us singing. And now Cynthia Asquith has turned up and if she sees me crying she will laugh her head off.

Cynthia is not my best friend any more ever since I told her what Aunty Celia said about the pot and the kettle.

We were having lunch which is like dinner only different, and Aunty Celia was telling Uncle Horace a story in sign language. They sometimes do that when they can't be bothered to go in his Study and Have a Word in Private. They do not know I can speak sign language, only Russian since Serena learned me that Da means Yes.

Aunty Celia began with the sign for Cynthia, which is *cuppy eye*, because of Cynthia's patch still being on her glasses.

So then *cuppy eye*'s mother, you know who she is, Horace – and then Aunty Celia made the sign of the *flicky hand*, which means Cynthia's mother because she is always flicking her long blonde hair about – went into his office *eyebrow squinty eye* and didn't come out for an hour!

Whose office? said Uncle Horace.

Piano fingers, of course. Are you listening to me?

Sadly, yes, said Uncle Horace.

Well, Janet says it's been going on for a year!

What has?

You know, *flicky hand, twisty shoulders, piano fingers, squinty eye.*

Which means: Cynthia's mother is having it off with Mr Lane the piano teacher.

That's nice, said Uncle Horace, because he hasn't really learned sign language, except for the *I am so bored* look he does sometimes.

Which is why *cuppy eye* is suddenly allowed in the choir! That child cannot sing a note. And to think *she's* never let me forget my little aberration!

No, said Uncle Horace, very weary, We mustn't forget your little aberration. That reminds me, I must show the new pool boy how the drain works.

Talk about the pot calling the kettle black, she said, And to think he only bought her that car last Christmas.

How on earth did he manage that? These teachers get paid far too much money, said Uncle Horace.

Not *piano fingers*, darling, her husband!

Do you think you'll have an affair if I buy you a new car, he said, all perky.

Ssh, she went, Not in front of the child, dear.

So when I told Cynthia and Cynthia told her mother, her mother said she must not play with me any more because I am a bad influence to say things like 'having it off' and then she telephoned Aunty Celia and they had a big row which was not in sign language. And now we are not best friends any more but Mortal Enemies.

I don't really want to be Mortal Enemies with Cynthia when I see her though, because she looks so sad in her patchy glasses and her old brown coat. I have got a new coat for the choir, it is red with a fur collar. And Geraint has got a new jacket which he has been Customising in his bedroom all night, which means he has made it look like a tramp's blazer. Aunty Celia will kill him when she sees it, he has ripped all the arm and tore off half the collar and he has put safety pins all down the front and took the buttons off and put badges there instead which say, Punk til you Puke and Bored Teenager and Sit on My Face.

Vicar is waiting outside the cathedral in a long dress like Dracula wears, with a bandage on his hand and, when he sees Geraint in his jacket and his shiny trousers, he says, Ah, Gerry, I see you're still not convinced by our little chat.

Because when we got back on the coach after the Demonstration we had to wait half an hour for Geraint and Jeffrey who Vicar said were Missing in Action. But when they came on the coach they stank of cider and B.O. and had snot all over their clothes and Jeffrey must have had an accident with his safety pin because a whole load of pimples on his cheek had burst and they were bleeding pus. They went and sat at the back and everyone was very happy about it because they did really stink.

I sat with Serena but only because she told Vicar I would be sick again, so he had to sit with Mrs PeePee and Nancy, and he got bit too, which is why he is wearing a bandage. I think he is a cissy because I got bit twice and I am not wearing even a plaster.

Vicar makes a big fuss getting us all In Position as he has had to have a Rethink because of Geraint's get-up and Jeffrey's new purple hair. He puts Geraint and Jeffrey behind Mrs PeePee who is right behind the old people who are behind the Muppet girls who are behind me and Cynthia. Serena has not turned up but Vicar has left a gap for her to stand next to him on the end. He says she is running in late.

Me and Cynthia have to be in the front because I am doing the Solo and Cynthia will take the plate round afterwards. I'm sad because I don't have a best friend now that Serena is missing so I give Cynthia the rollie eyes when Vicar bores on with his instructions but it doesn't work. Then I go, Cyn, Cyn, he is like Count Dracula – Ah, New Blood! and I show my teeth at her like fangs but that doesn't work too. She won't even speak back, so when we have warm-up before they let the crowds in and sing 'Silent

Night, Holy Night', I sing to her some new words:

Cyn-th-ia Ass-quith,

Will you be, My friend, A-gain?

And she starts giggling and goes:

What abou-out, If mu-um finds out?

And I go:

We can keep it a see-e-e-cret

Nobod-ee-ee will e-ever know,

Sleep in Heavenly Pea-eece! Slee-eep in Heavenly Peace!

Then they open the doors for the Congregation, which is like all the old people in the world with a million sticks and rainhats.

Uncle Horace is easy to tell because according to Geraint he has got Grecian hair, that is why it is quite black. Plus, he is with Aunty Celia who has got a massive hat on shaped like a lady's umbrella from the old days. She does a walk very near Mrs Asquith, so I think she is going to ask her if they can be best friends again, but when she gets really close up she does a huff with her shoulder and marches the other way. Some adults are very childish.

I'm looking for my dad but he hasn't come. In all the best stories, the dad turns up at the end and it's Happy Ever After, but that never happens in real life, only sometimes on television. And that starts me thinking about when we all played *Little House on the Prairie* for the Social Worker and my mother put on her best long dress and brought a loaf of bread from the baker's and put it in the oven so she could take it out when the Social Worker came. And my dad came back from the Bookies in the middle of the visit with his face all black because he'd gone in the coal shed first and made it dirty, and we all sat round like it was just normal to have a dad with a black face and home-made bread.

I'm wishing we could do *Little House on the Prairie* again when Cynthia nudges me because Vicar is waving like mad with his bandage fingers. I do my Solo which is alright and then I sit back down again and I am fed up. I don't want a pony or a dog or a Bionic Woman for Christmas. What I really want for Christmas is my mam.

Twenty

It is snowing! It is snowing! I cannot believe my eyes!

When everybody is going away and we are the last because we have to wait, Cynthia goes, Enid look! and points to the big doorway in the church and it is snowing massive snow outside. We do a run straight out of the church and round the circle in the middle of the front and we are all white in one second.

Then Cynthia goes, Enid, look! Serena's got a boyfriend! and she points to where we ran out and Serena is standing by the church door smoking a fag and talking to a man who is a man just like my dad. Then I go close up to spy on them and I think that must be my dad because he is wearing his leathers and has got a fag in his face but he has not got a beard, so I think it can't be my dad. Then he turns round and goes,

Forgotten me already, Pumpkin?

And it is my dad.

*

I am sitting in the front of the Rover on all the plastics and every time I move it sounds like a fart. Uncle Horace says, Don't do that, old chum, when Geraint puts the window down in the back, and then Uncle Horace fiddles with the knobs on the front and the air blows in all over my face. When I turn round and stick my tongue out at Geraint I see he is looking quite green like sprouts which we are having for dinner.

Aunty Celia goes, Horace, pull over for a second, dear, and then Geraint opens the door and he is sick all over the road. It looks like brown porridge on the snow. It is the best Christmas present ever.

My dad is coming back on his own because he is on a Motorbike, that is why he is wearing his leathers. After we had a cuddle at the church, he said to Serena, This is my daughter Enid, and she said, I know, we're already acquainted, Privyet, milaya moya, and I said, Privyet Serena, which means Hello in Russian.

My dad looked really chuffed that I could speak languages and then he said to Serena, Can I give you a lift somewhere? and she went, No thanks, I'm cool, which she always says when she is giving someone the brush-off. Then he said to me, I'll meet you back at the ranch, honey. Bet I get there before you.

How much? I said, because that's what my mother always used to ask when they had a Wager, and he thought for a second and then he went, A quid. See you in a flea.

A whole quid! I can buy everyone loads of presents now. While I'm sitting on the plastics going home, I think about what to get them. I will get Aunty Celia a new hairbrush and maybe a pinny because she burnt a hole in hers at Harvest Festival time and has not wore it since, and a new glove because I lost one of her old ones. I will get Uncle Horace a trumpet because he is always playing his lips like a trumpet and singing sometimes, especially when he is in the downstairs bathroom. My dad is easy; I will get him the parrot from Gordon's pet stall and a big bag of Old Holborn for his tin. Geraint is very difficult. Then I have the brilliant idea about what to get him. I will get him some new underpants.

Except that at this rate Geraint will get a Big Fat Nothing because he keeps making us stop so that he can be sick. We must have stopped seventeen times already, but as soon as Uncle Horace gets going fast, he goes Uh-uuhh, in the back and Aunty Celia goes, Uh-oh, Horace, pull over will you?

It is still snowing when we come down the hill but my dad is there already standing under the hedge and lighting a fag. We all pile out but Geraint first because he has to be sick again in the bush, and Aunty Celia goes, You must have gone like the wind, Carlo, and he goes, Yeah, Ceel, white-lining all the way.

Then he grabs me and tickles me and goes, Where's my quid, Tinker?

I haven't got any money apart from my savings which are thirty-seven pee, so I go, Double or quits, which he always says when he loses, and he says, Righto, I call the next bet.

Then Uncle Horace goes to put the car indoors and he says, Carlo, old boy, don't tell me you came all the way from Cardiff on this? and he is pointing into the garage and when I go to see, I see it is Mrs Mickey's scooter.

Goes like a peach, says my dad, Got nearly sixty out of her on the A39.

You won't be going back tonight though, surely, Carlo? says Aunty Celia, with her eyelashes going like a moth, Because we'd love you to stay, wouldn't we, Horace? Horace?

My Uncle Horace is not listening because he's trying to get his leg over the scooter the wrong way.

I used to have one of these in the 'fifties, he says, and my dad goes, It's probably the same one, Hor.

But he shakes his head and has gone all sweaty and gets off trying to get on and goes, No it was a Vespa Douglas. What a dream!

Geraint is having a moody over by the wall, so we all go indoors and Aunty Celia says, I think this calls for a little Celebration, which is Morse code for everyone having a gin and tonic and some peanuts.

Twenty-one

Sapphire Street
25th December 1976

O Come on all the Faithfuls, Joyful n Triumphungh, o, nuhhnuhh, o nuhhhnuh to Belalalah! Come and nnn-nuh, Born the King of nn-n-

Enid, come here a sec. Get rid of that racket, love.

My father is in the kitchen doing something Top Secret which is actually trying to squash the turkey in the oven, so I take the ten pees from him and go and give them to the Carol Singer at our front door. It is not a Carol Singer, it is Robert Crumb wearing a tinsel ring on his head. No wonder it was so rubbish.

Then I go back inside because I want to have another try of making a fire with my new magnifying glass, which is the best part of my Spy Kit. In it there is a black badge which says SPY in red, as if you would ever wear it and let everyone know you were a spy! Then there's a disguise which is a nose and glasses and moustache all stuck together, and there's also a pen that writes invisible that has gone missing.

My dad got me very worried this morning when he said, Merry Christmas, Enid, Surprise! and covered my eyes and started taking me outside. I thought, Oh no, he has gone and got me a dog! I am gone off dogs but I forgot to tell him. But it wasn't a dog, it was Aunty Celia and Uncle Horace and Geraint and they were standing in the garden with their scarves all matching pretending to be snowmen. Then when we came inside I said, It's okay, Uncle Horace, you can stop pretending now, and tried to take the pipe out of his mouth, and he went, Enid, you are a Wonder. This is my Christmas present from Aunty Celia.

And Aunty Celia said, He won't light it, Carlo, don't worry, and my dad went, No worries, Ceel, just all of you relax now, okay? Leave everything to me.

And she looked at him like he was Cliff Richard who she adores and she said, You are an absolute angel, Carlo. Don't suppose you've got any ice?

They are all wearing the same jumpers that Aunty Celia's sister has sent them for Christmas, and she has sent one for me as well. I thought it had got a dog on the front but Geraint went, No, it's supposed to be a reindeer.

Geraint has Customise his jumper by making big holes in it and ripping the sleeves off and wearing a check shirt underneath.

Uncle Horace has Customise his jumper as well by spilling egg all down it so only Aunty Celia has got a picture on hers. That looks like a dog too.

When I go back in after telling Robert Crumb he is a terrible singer and to clear off, Aunty Celia is looking out of the window. Robert Crumb has not gone away, he is swinging on our gate. She says, Oh dear, poor, poor boy. Do you think he's an orphan of the Parish? Should we invite him in to play, Enid?

And I go, No chance, he only lives two doors down and he is a little tyke and a cur!

Aunty Celia goes, That's not very charitable, is it, now? What would Jesus do?

Then my dad comes in from the kitchen and sticks his head under the nets and goes, Robert Crumb get off that bloody gate before I brain you! Sorry, Ceel, did you want a top-up? And she forgets all about Robert Crumb and goes, Oh Lovely, Carlo. Do you need a hand in the kitchen while Horace has his little snooze? I'm really quite an accomplished cook!

Uncle Horace is wearing my Spy disguise to disguise him being asleep but it is obvious because behind it he is snoring and a bit of dribble is hanging off his mouth. Geraint gives me the sign language of *creased-up face* which means: I Am So Ashamed of My Family, and then he goes, Enid?

I go, Ye-es, all suspicious,

You don't want that badge do you?

And I go, What badge?

And he goes, That SPY one.

And I go, What, this one with SPY on it? and I hold it up and study it with my magnifying glass.

And he goes, That one, yes – only really quiet like he is going to lose his temper any second which is fine by me. But then I remember it is Christmas and my mother always says you must have Peace and Good Will to All Men even if he is your Nemesis and Waste of Space, and I don't want the stupid badge anyway so I say, Well, I might. That all depends.

And he goes, I'll trade you if you really don't want it. How about this one?

He is pointing at his Customise jumper with the badge on it of the Sexy Pistols who are my new favourite pop group in the whole world. And I have a think a minute to keep him in suspense and then I spit on my hand and hold it out for a shake and I go,

Deal!

Geraint, son of Erbin

a synopsis

Gwenhyfar is riding to join Arthur in a hunt near Caerllion ar Wysg when she sees Geraint son of Erbin, heading there too. Travelling together they meet a huge knight, riding with a dwarf and a young woman. Gwenhyfar's maid asks the dwarf who the knight is, but he hits her across the face with his whip. The same thing happens with Geraint. Determined to avenge the insult, Geraint seeks armour in the next town (now called Caerdydd).

Arriving at the castle he sees next to it a dilapidated hall. In the hall are an elderly couple in shabby silks and their beautiful daughter, in worn-out clothes. They take Geraint in and explain how they lost their wealth to a nephew who now rules the castle. He also discovers there is a jousting tournament the next day, and that the knight he is pursuing has come to defend his title. The elderly man offers him armour, and Geraint asks if he can fight for the love of their daughter. They agree and Geraint triumphs. He sends the injured knight, Edern, son of Nudd, to Arthur's court to beg forgiveness from Gwenhyfar.

The Earl of the castle agrees to repay the elderly man, Earl Ynywl, all he has lost. They bring him food and clothing, but Geraint asks that their daughter stay in her old smock until they reach Arthur's court where Gwenhyfar can dress her.

Edern arrives at court, is forgiven and tended. The next day Geraint arrives with Earl Ynywl's daughter, Enid. They are welcomed; Gwenhyfar dresses Enid and Arthur gives her to Geraint. Enid becomes very popular at court while Geraint thrives on his love of hard combat.

After several years Geraint hears that his father is ailing and enemies are threatening his kingdom in Cornwall. Geraint reluctantly returns to defend his lands across the Hafren, but continues to fight in tournaments until his fame spreads. Having achieved this, Geraint begins to stay with Enid until there is nothing he would rather do than be alone in their chamber with her. Eventually Geraint's nobles and court start to resent this. Erbin tells Enid this and she is distressed that Geraint should lose his fame because of her. Waking, Geraint hears her tears but thinks that she wants him to go and fight because she loves someone else.

He takes his horse and armour, leaves the court, and makes Enid ride in front of him. He tells her not to turn back whatever happens. He also forbids her to speak unless he speaks to her. They travel on wild roads and three times Enid overhears knights plotting to attack them. Each time she warns Geraint. He is angry with her for speaking and refuses to believe she is concerned about him. He kills the knights and orders Enid to continue as before, threatening to punish her if she speaks. She promises to do her best to obey him. They spend the night in the forest, but Enid speaks to Geraint again when he wakes.

The next day they are given lodgings in a town. The Earl of the house begs Enid to stay with him, but she refuses and, waking Geraint, warns him they must leave. They are pursued by a host of knights but Enid sees them coming and warns Geraint again. He is furious that she will not hold her tongue. Geraint fells eighty knights, and they carry on until they come to a valley where Geraint fights a knight named Y Brenin Bychan. Defeating him he makes him swear loyalty. The knight agrees and asks Geraint to stay and be healed, but Geraint refuses and they go on until they meet with Arthur's hunt. Arthur insists Geraint stays for treatment, while Enid is tended by Gwenhyfar. But as soon as he is fit, Geraint continues his journey, with Enid ahead of him as before.

They meet a lady crying over a dead knight who was attacked by three giants. Geraint pursues the giants and kills them but is wounded. When he returns, he collapses. They are rescued by an Earl who takes Geraint to his court on a stretcher. The earl wants Enid to stay with him if Geraint dies, and when she refuses him he hits her. Hearing her scream, Geraint comes to, and kills the earl. He looks at Enid and is sorry, realising she has been in the right.

They leave on the same horse and meet Y Brenin Bychan who finds them shelter until Geraint is healed. Then they travel on, Enid happy and content, until they come to a fork in the road. One road leads to a hedge of mist and enchanted games. Geraint enters the mist, although no one has ever come out alive. Once inside he is challenged by a knight, whom he defeats. The knight agrees to lift the mist and enchantment and Geraint returns, much to Enid's relief. Everyone is reconciled and Geraint and Enid go back to their kingdom which Geraint rules bravely and successfully, and where there is admiration for him and Enid evermore.

Synopsis by Penny Thomas
for the full story see *The Mabinogion, A New Translation*
by Sioned Davies (Oxford World's Classics, 2007).

Afterword

There's an old Welsh proverb which declares: 'Be she old, or be she young, a woman's strength is in her tongue.'

Growing up in the 1970s as the youngest of six daughters, it seemed to me back then that – if my mother was any example – a woman's strength lay in her ability to cook, clean, iron, mend, do four different jobs, and still find the energy to play with her children, plait their hair, listen to their grievances and adjudicate in arguments: and there were quite a few of those. If my mother had no time for quarrelling, us girls made up for it in spades. Even now, the catchphrases of our junior years still ring in my ears: from the universal 'It's not fair', and the non-negotiable 'No deal, Buster', to the evocative, economical, 'You're dead.'

So when I was invited to reimagine one of the tales from the *Mabinogion*, the story of Geraint and Enid immediately 'spoke' to me. A seemingly straightforward romance, it features a husband and wife whose relationship gets into difficulties. Geraint is a rich and powerful knight, Enid a beautiful maiden, both of whom – through a misunderstanding on his part – undergo a long journey and together face a number of trials before finally conquering a range of assorted enemies and their own personal difficulties.

But it wasn't the marital entanglement or the perilous journey – which resulted in Enid saving the day – that attracted me. It was the opportunity to explore the idea of the female voice as powerful, as a tool – as a weapon. I also wanted to utilise some of the more traditional fairy tale elements of the story and locate them in a light-hearted and modern setting. It is Enid who embodies the essence of the traditional fairy tale, but who has the most unusual role in the narrative. In the original tale, Geraint, misunderstanding Enid's words, believes she is about to be unfaithful; as a punishment he takes her on a gruelling trek across the countryside during which he will prove his manhood and fighting prowess, and punish her for her seeming infidelity. Not only does he command her to 'clothe thee in the worst riding-dress that thou has in thy possession', he puts her in charge of the ever-increasing spoils of his victories – numerous horses and wagon-loads of armour – and then complains when he sees how difficult it is for her to manage this task. But his cruellest punishment is enforcing her silence:

'And whatever thou mayest see, and whatever thou mayest hear concerning me,' he says, 'do thou not turn back. And unless I speak unto thee, say not thou one word either.'

As it turns out, it's also the least effective punishment, because despite this interdiction, Enid so loves her boorish husband that – even on pain of death – she disobeys him whenever she realises he might be in danger. This leads to a series of increasingly comic exchanges where the exasperated – but perpetually saved – Geraint keeps telling Enid to be quiet.

After the first time she warns him, he admonishes her: 'Say not one word unto me, unless I speak first unto thee. And I declare unto Heaven, if thou doest not thus, it will be to thy cost.'

Enid demurely replies: 'I will do, as far as I can, Lord.'

It's the '*as far as I can*', which is telling here; it's Enid's get-out-of-jail card and she's not afraid to use it: '*as far as I am able, Lord*', she says, and again, '*I will, Lord, while I can.*'

His command for her silence and her 'silent' refusal to obey is at the heart of what Vladimir Propp, in his study of Russian fairy tales, describes as the 'violation of an interdiction'.

Greek myth, fairy tales, modern literature and horror films are full of such interdictions: don't look back, don't stray from the path, don't open the door, don't pick up phone... and for Enid, it was: *don't speak*. This particular interdiction harks back to the bible: 'Let your women keep silence... for it is not permitted unto them to speak' (Corinthians); and it resonates through our culture, from the medieval Scold's Bridle right up to the recent tirade of verbal abuse heaped upon feminist and women's rights activist Sandra Fluke by the Republican 'talk radio' host Rush Limbaugh. His attempt to negate her right to speak through slander and ridicule on the airwaves might be seen as the 21st century way to silence a woman's voice. In the voice lies power. All around the world, from Lincoln to Liberia, oppressed groups and organisations use the word 'voice' to convey a sense of unity against discrimination, a sense of identity and of solidarity in the face of enforced aphony.

I have written about so-called 'elective' mutism before: but in Geraint and Enid, the whole point of the story is that Enid's voice is a potent force which cannot be silenced: silence will result in death. I wanted to explore the voice as innocent, unflinching, but also without guile. And for me the most immediate way to do this was to write in the voice of a child; to reveal her thoughts, her questions, and her assertions.

Although my Geraint and Enid are cousins and far from romantically attached, and even though the story is set in 1976, I wanted to retain some of the architecture of the tale. So Geraint is a rich, spoilt public schoolboy who lives in a mansion in Devon, and Enid is from a council house in Splott. Enid takes an enforced 'journey' in the sense that she goes to stay in Devon while her mother is in hospital, and she has many trials and challenges to undergo throughout her stay (some inflicted by her cousin, but many of her own invention). But more pressing was my intention to explore a liminal space: the spiritual and emotional wilderness of loss and grief: not just of wandering through unknown territory, but of rendering the inarticulacy of childhood longing in simple terms, with all the misunderstanding and humour that might entail.

In the original legend, Enid does a lot more listening than she does talking, and what she hears allows her to save Geraint time and again. So, my Enid is obsessed with becoming a spy, one of the Champions, perhaps, or Wonderwoman. And like the original Enid, she can't help but say things she really shouldn't. Neither could be described as 'passive' characters by any means: the original Enid's dilemma was an emotional one – whether to speak or be silent – but, to rephrase the cliché – her words spoke louder than actions. In my interpretation, Enid's quest is similar: to negotiate the strangeness of the world she's found herself in, and for her, the natural way to do that is to question everything. So, when Geraint commands her to obey him 'upon pain of death', Enid instantly agrees and then violates his interdiction at the first opportunity.

Other echoes of the original tale cried out for modification: the darkly comic episodes – when Geraint is challenged to kill three, then four, then five horsemen, then a clatter of knights, then a few giants – are transformed into boyhood obsessions: becoming an instant expert on ants or the movement of the tides or left-wing politics; laboriously constructing a Skylab model (a quest that may take a lifetime); discovering and therefore knowing absolutely everything there is to know about punk rock...

And even though 'my' Enid may question everything, I wanted her to retain an element of her namesake's eloquent silence; so she refuses to 'spill the beans' when faced with an interrogation, and has the insight to 'save' Geraint by *not* speaking up. But I also wanted to show the 'mists vanishing' from their relationship, and to suggest a future where they might meet with equanimity.

And, of course, remembering how difficult it is for the younger child to ever win the battle, I wanted Enid to have the last word.

Trezza Azzopardi

Acknowledgements

I'd like to thank Seren for giving me the opportunity to take part in this series, and especially Penny Thomas for her help and advice.

I'm indebted to my family and friends for reading, inspiration and kindness.

NEW STORIES FROM THE
MABINOGION

OWEN SHEERS: WHITE RAVENS

Two stories, two different times, but the thread of an ancient tale runs through the lives of twenty-first-century farmer's daughter Rhian and the mysterious Branwen… Wounded in Italy, Matthew O'Connell is seeing out WWII in a secret government department spreading rumours and myths to the enemy. But when he's given the task of escorting a box containing six raven chicks from a remote hill farm in Wales to the Tower of London, he becomes part of a story over which he seems to have no control.

RUSSELL CELYN JONES: THE NINTH WAVE

Pwyll, a young Welsh ruler in a post-oil world, finds his inherited status hard to take. And he's never quite sure how he's drawn into murdering his future wife's fiancé, losing his only son and switching beds with the king of the underworld. In this bizarrely upside-down, medieval world of the near future, life is cheap and the surf is amazing; but you need a horse to get home again down the M4.

GWYNETH LEWIS: THE MEAT TREE

A dangerous tale of desire, DNA, incest and flowers plays out within the wreckage of an ancient spaceship in *The Meat Tree*, an absorbing retelling of one of the best-known Welsh myths by prizewinning writer and poet, Gwyneth Lewis.

An elderly investigator and his female apprentice hope to extract the fate of the ship's crew from its antiquated virtual reality game system, but their empirical approach falters as the story tangles with their own imagination.

NEW STORIES FROM THE MABINOGION

LLOYD JONES: SEE HOW THEY RUN

Small-minded academic Dr Llwyd McNamara has a grant to research Wales' biggest hero, rugby star Dylan Manawydan Jones – Big M. But as the doctor plays with USB sticks in his office, the gods have other plans...

Llwyd discovers a link between Big M and his own life at the luxurious but strange Hotel Corvo. But from here things only get stranger. Are claims to a link between Big M and the Celtic myths of the past just a load of academic waffle... and what is the significance of the mouse tattoo?

CYNAN JONES: BIRD, BLOOD, SNOW

"No matter how you build them, the world will come crashing against your fences."

Hoping to give him a better start, Peredur's mother takes him from the estates. But when local kids cycle into his life he heads after them, accompanied by the notion of finding Arthur – an absent, imaginary guardian. Used to making up his own worlds, he's something of a joke. Until he seriously maims one of the older kids. And that's when the trouble starts.

TISHANI DOSHI: FOUNTAINVILLE

Gang wars, opium dreams and a mysterious clinic where women are voluntarily confined are all part of the landscape in remote borderland town Fountainville.

But when Owain Knight arrives from across the sea his entanglement with Begum, the owner of the town's mythical fountain, her mobster husband Kedar and her assistant Luna spells a terrible change for them all.